RA

ASCENT TO THE SUN

STING OF THE SCORPION

THE WRATH OF RA

CAROLE WILKINSON

Catnip

CATNIP BOOKS
Published by Catnip Publishing Ltd.
14 Greville Street
London
EC1N 8SB

This edition published 2008
1 3 5 7 9 10 8 6 4 2

Ramose: Sting of the Scorpion and *Ramose: The Wrath of Ra* first
published in Australia by black dog books, 71 Gertrude Street,
Fitzroy Vic 3065

Ramose: Sting of the Scorpion copyright © Carole Wilkinson 2001
Ramose: The Wrath of Ra copyright © Carole Wilkinson 2002

A CIP catalogue record for this book is available from the British
Library

ISBN 978-1-84647-042-4

Printed in Poland

www.catnippublishing.co.uk

CONTENTS

RAMOSE: STING OF THE SCORPION

RAMOSE: THE WRATH OF RA

RAMOSE

STING OF THE SCORPION

NIGHT IN THE DESERT

"**P**OOR MERY is hungry," said Karoya, stroking her cat. She threw the last pat of donkey dung on the spluttering fire. "She shouldn't be cold as well." The sandy-coloured cat sat as close to the flames as she could without burning her fur.

"We're all hungry," said Hapu grumpily. "But you're more concerned about that cat than us."

"We chose to be here. She didn't," said Karoya.

"Well, if we were travelling along the river we wouldn't be hungry," grumbled Hapu. "We could fish every day."

Ramose's stomach growled. Like the others he had eaten nothing but stale bread and dried figs for the last three days.

"We can't go back to the river, Hapu," said Ramose. "It's too dangerous."

Three days earlier, Ramose had seen men searching the riverbank. He was sure it was the vizier's men looking for them.

"We crossed over the river so that they couldn't find us," complained Hapu. "I don't see why we have to travel in the desert as well."

Ramose had insisted that they leave the fertile Nile Valley and walk parallel to the river but out of sight of the fertile land.

"We attract too much attention," Ramose said. "In Egypt everyone has a job to do, a place to be. Three young people shouldn't be wandering around the country by themselves."

Hapu grunted. He knew Ramose was right.

Ramose stared moodily into the fire. The flames were dying. A handful of reeds and a pat of donkey dung didn't burn for long. He saw a slight movement out of the corner of his eye. As he watched, a pale, creamy coloured scorpion crawled out from under a rock. It was big—more than a palm-width long. It climbed onto the rock and raised its pincers. Its tail curled menacingly above it. Ramose was about to reach out and squash it with his sandal. Then he realised that the creature was warming itself by the fire just as they were. He left it alone.

It was a strange situation for a prince to be in, travelling on foot, hiding in the desert, living like a barbarian. There was a reason why he was doing it though—a good reason. He was going back to the royal palace at Thebes. He had to let his father know that he was still alive. Then he would reclaim his place as Pharaoh's elder son and heir to the throne of Egypt.

It was over a year since one of his father's lesser wives had tried to poison him so that her own son, Tuthmosis, could become pharaoh. Ramose's tutor and nanny had saved him by pretending that he had died. They had hidden him in the tomb makers' village where he lived, as a scribe, for many months.

Karoya was roasting a snake over the tiny fire. That was to be their evening meal.

"I don't see why anybody would choose to live out here," grumbled Hapu. "Why didn't your people live in villages?" he asked Karoya. "Were they running away from someone?"

"No," said Karoya indignantly. "It was the life they chose."

Karoya was the only one who liked travelling close to the desert. It reminded her of her home in Kush, a desert country to the south of Egypt, which had been conquered during Pharaoh's last military campaign.

"But how did you survive?"

"My people knew the desert as well as Egyptians know the river. We kept herds of cattle. We were always moving, seeking grass for the cattle to eat. It was a good life."

Karoya was speaking as if her people didn't exist any more. Ramose knew that she had been captured by his father's army and forced to become a slave. He had never asked her what had happened to her family. He was afraid that the answer would make him ashamed of being Egyptian.

Karoya handed them each a piece of the snake and a gourd of water.

"It's like eating leather," grumbled Hapu, spitting out bits of snakeskin.

The snake was tough and tasteless, but Ramose didn't complain.

He glanced over at the black-skinned slave girl sitting next to him. Without Karoya's knowledge of the desert, Ramose knew they would have died of hunger. Their food supplies had been scanty, but what little they had, Karoya found. She had killed the snake. She had trapped a bird. She organised night-time trips back into the fringes of the cultivated land to collect water, grain and vegetables. Ramose didn't like adding to his crimes by stealing from people's fields and orchards. But they had no choice. He hoped Maat, the goddess of justice, would understand. He promised himself he would make an offering to her as soon as he could.

Hapu didn't know anything about the desert, but he was a loyal friend and good company. He told stories as they walked. Even when Ramose was feeling like he'd never achieve his goal, Hapu could always make him smile. Without his friends, Ramose may well have given up in despair.

"It's your turn to go and get water," Karoya said to Ramose.

Ramose nodded. He no longer thought it strange that a prince should do as a slave girl told him. Back in the palace, servants weren't even allowed to look him in the eye, let alone tell him what to do.

He took the water-skin and walked towards the fertile land. Thoth, the moon god, hadn't risen yet, but Ramose used the stars to guide him. It took him an hour to reach the first fields of the cultivated land. He found an irrigation canal surrounding a field of beans. He filled the water-skin and picked some beans as well.

By the time he got back to the camp, his friends were asleep. They had arranged their reed mats around the little fireplace—even though the fire had gone out. Karoya was wrapped in the length of faded cloth that she wore over her head. She was curled around Mery for extra warmth. Hapu only had a coarse linen shirt. Ramose wrapped himself in the woollen cloak that had been with him ever since he left the palace. It wasn't enough to keep out the cold of the desert night.

Two hours later, Ramose was still awake. The sand was as hard as a block of stone. He turned onto his back and stared up at the night sky. The stars in their millions twinkled above him.

In his head, Ramose ran through the events of the past weeks again and again. If he'd done things differently they wouldn't be in such a miserable state. A month ago, a high priest had accused them of being tomb robbers and tried to arrest them. They could easily have been imprisoned in Memphis. They'd had a narrow escape.

A wave of shame and anger crept over Ramose. The truth was, he was a tomb robber. He had stolen gold and jewels from Pharaoh Senusret's pyramid. It was the worst crime in Egypt and he was guilty of it. It hadn't been Ramose's choice, though. A gang of tomb robbers had kidnapped him and they had forced him to crawl into the heart of the pyramid and steal the gold and jewels from the tomb. Hapu had fallen into their clutches as well. The two boys had been abandoned, trapped underground. Mery had saved them. The cat had led them out of the tomb.

He was sure Vizier Wersu was pursuing them because they were tomb robbers. The vizier didn't know it was Ramose who had robbed the tomb. He, like everyone else, thought that Ramose was dead. That was the way Ramose wanted it to stay.

Ramose removed a sharp stone from under his back. He sighed and turned on his other side. He felt something prick his leg. He shifted again with annoyance. Would he ever get to sleep?

As he lay there, a swarm of mosquitoes suddenly attacked him. He couldn't see them, but he could feel them biting him all over. Then a tall, thin man with a face like a crocodile appeared from nowhere. He had his long, white robes draped over one arm as he walked. Even in the darkness, Ramose knew who it was. It was Vizier Wersu. He was holding a bronze statue of Seth in the form of a strange animal with square ears, a pointed snout and a forked tail. Seth was the god of chaos and confusion who had killed his own brother, Osiris, and gouged out the eye of his nephew, Horus, god of the sky.

Seth was an ugly-looking god, but the statue was a beautiful thing. Ramose thought about the cost of such a large bronze statue. It was probably enough to feed three families for a year. He wondered why anyone would want to worship such an unpleasant god. He admired the delicately carved hippopotamuses around the base. It's strange how you can see so much detail in dreams, thought Ramose. And odd how you can feel as well as see. He scratched furiously at the itchy bites all over his body.

The vizier had an evil look in his eye. He took hold of the feet of Seth with both hands and swung the statue as if it were a weapon. It was a weapon. He swung the heavy bronze statue again, aiming it right at Ramose. Ramose rolled out of the way and the statue dug into the sand, narrowly missing his head. He was surprised at the skinny vizier's strength. The vizier raised the statue above his head. Ramose tried to roll out of the way, but he caught his foot in his bag. Vizier Wersu brought down the statue hard on his right leg. It hurt. Ramose cried out in pain.

Then Ramose saw that in his other hand, the vizier held a large fig, the biggest fig Ramose had ever seen. Wersu was trying to force it into Ramose's mouth. Ramose tried to stop him, but he couldn't move because his leg was hurting and his body was itching from the mosquito bites. Wersu hit his leg again with the bronze statue. The pain was terrible. Ramose opened his mouth to scream and the vizier prised open Ramose's jaws and forced the fig in. The huge fruit wedged in his mouth so that he could neither spit it out nor swallow it.

It was cold, so cold. Ramose shivered and shivered and couldn't stop. He felt sick. This is a dream, he told himself. All I have to do is wake up. His eyes were wide open but he couldn't wake up.

The moon god, Thoth, finally climbed into the sky. Ramose was pleased to see the bright disc of the moon. Thoth was also the ibis-headed god of writing, worshipped by scribes. Thoth was only there for a moment before the black sky turned dark orange. The first rays of the sun were appearing over the horizon. Before long the sky was light and the moon faded until it was like a ghost of itself in the morning sky.

Karoya awoke and sat up. Hapu stirred in his sleep. Ramose realised with a jolt that he wasn't dreaming. He was awake. The pain in his leg from Wersu's blow was unbearable. The itching hadn't gone away. And try as he might, he could not swallow the fig jammed into his mouth. He tried to speak to Karoya, but he could only make a terrible animal noise.

Karoya knelt down at his side. Her forehead was creased with concern. She seemed to be shuddering and quivering from side to side. Then

Ramose realised that it was him that was moving. He was shivering violently and couldn't stop.

"Hapu," said Karoya. "Quick, get the water."

Hapu sat up sleepily. As soon as he saw Ramose he jumped to his feet.

"What's happened to him?"

"I don't know, but he needs water. His tongue is so swollen, it looks like he might choke."

What's wrong with me? Ramose wanted to ask as he gulped the water, but he couldn't. He had never felt so sick. He was sweating as if he were lying out in the midday sun, but the sun's rays hadn't yet reached their camp. He couldn't breathe properly. He sucked in gulps of air. His heart was pounding. Karoya was swimming blurredly in front of him.

Ramose felt her hands as she searched his body for signs of injury or illness. She touched his right leg and he cried out in pain.

"Here," said Karoya. "Look. Something has bitten him."

Karoya pulled the cloak away from him. Ramose raised his heavy head and glimpsed his lower leg, which was swollen to the size of a melon. He might have imagined the vizier hitting him with a statue, but the pain was real.

Karoya suddenly snatched up her grinding stone. Ramose flinched as she held it above her head ready to hurl at him. He tried to cry out again. Not you, Karoya. You haven't turned against me, have you? No sound came out, but saliva dribbled from his mouth as if he were a baby. He felt a rush of air as the stone narrowly missed his leg and dug into the sand next to him. What is happening? he wanted to ask. Ramose felt his eyelids droop. His life was in danger, he didn't know what was real and what wasn't, but all he wanted to do was sleep. Karoya knelt down and picked up something very cautiously between her fingers. Ramose's vision was blurry, but he could make out what it was. It was a dead scorpion.

2

SAND AND MIRRORS

RAMOSE OPENED his eyes. A man with a thin, grim face and a small, straight mouth was looking down at him.

For a moment, Ramose thought that it was Wersu. Then he realised that the face was burnt dark brown and creased like old leather. It was framed by a piece of dark cloth wrapped around the man's head. His black, piercing eyes were bright like a bird's, nothing like the vizier's. As the man reached across to feel Ramose's brow, the boy felt the coarse cloth of a thick, long-sleeved garment scrape against his arm. The man smelt bad, as if he had not bathed for a very long time.

The pain in Ramose's leg was still there, but he wasn't itchy any more. The man held a gourd to Ramose's mouth. Ramose drank from it. The liquid was thick and tasted something like milk, but it was nothing like the milk from cattle or gazelles. It tasted like someone's feet had been washed in it.

Then the man disappeared from Ramose's view. He heard an unintelligible shout and then felt movement. His body was jolted and jarred, as if he were lying on something that was being dragged along the ground.

A piece of coarse, hairy cloth was stretched above him to provide shade from the sun. He could feel the warmth penetrating the cloth. Ramose turned his head to see where he was. Under the edges of the shade cloth he could see nothing but sand.

There was a strong animal smell, so unpleasant it made him feel sick. All around him were animal noises—some that sounded familiar, others that didn't sound like any animal he'd ever known. There were other unfamiliar sounds, irregular clinkings and clankings. His body rocked and lurched as he was pulled along by something unseen.

Ramose was comfortable, despite all the bumping and the smells. He could feel a strong, cool pressure on his right leg, as if there were something heavy weighing down on it. The pain was still there, but it seemed to be somewhere else, as if someone had taken it out and put it down at a distance.

Ramose didn't know where he was going or who was taking him there, but at that moment he didn't care.

He woke again. He was still bumping along. He smelt the strong smell of fresh animal dung. He heard voices, strange sounds made in the back of the throat. The voices made no sense, though. The unknown animal joined in. Ramose tried to sit up but he couldn't. Then the movement stopped. Everything was still.

The shade cloth was suddenly thrown back and there stood Karoya. She was looking down at him with the same crinkled look of concern as when he'd last seen her. Ramose's tongue had shrunk back to something like normal size. He thought he would try and speak.

"Hello, Karoya." His words were a little slurry, but Karoya's black face was suddenly split by a brilliant white crescent as she smiled down at him.

"How are you feeling?" she asked.

"Better," he said. "I saw a strange man."

"That was Zeyd."

Ramose tried to sit up, but couldn't move his arms or legs. He raised his head and saw the reason why he was unable to move. He was tied to a sort of sled.

"Have we been captured by barbarians?" he asked.

Karoya smiled again as she undid the knots. "No. You are tied onto the sled, so you don't fall off."

He looked up past Karoya's bent head and saw what had been pulling his sled.

"I must be still dreaming," he said, as he stared at the strangest creature he had seen in his entire life.

"No, you're not," said Karoya, as she helped him to sit up.

Ramose stared at the creature. It was the biggest animal he'd ever seen. It towered above him. It had large hoofed feet, skinny legs and matted brown hair. On the end of a long, curved neck was the ugliest face imaginable. A big-lipped mouth full of large, yellow teeth moved from side to side as it chewed on some dried grass. Strangest of all, on the creature's back was a large hump.

"What is that?" asked Ramose, unable to tear his eyes away from the ugly creature.

"It is called a camel," said Karoya knowledge-ably, holding a gourd of milk to Ramose's lips.

"Why does the milk taste so strange?" he asked.

"It's camel's milk."

As Ramose sipped the milk, he looked around and took in his new surroundings. He didn't have to ask where they were—he could see. They were deep in the desert. Whichever way he looked he could see nothing but sand.

It was not the desert along the edges of the fertile land that he and his friends had been travelling in. There were no rocky outcrops, no occasional tufts of grass. There was no sound of insects, no birds flying overhead. In every direction all he could see was sand—hard flat sand and its surface rippled like a wind-blown pond.

A group of grubby children was standing star-ing at Ramose.

Ramose whispered to Karoya. "Are you sure we aren't captives?"

Karoya laughed. "No, we are guests. Honoured guests. These people are nomads. Zeyd is their chief. They travel from oasis to oasis to graze their goats. And you don't have to whisper, Ramose. They have their own language and they don't understand a word of Egyptian."

"How do you know so much about them? Can you speak their language?"

"I don't have to speak to them," said Karoya, laughing again. "This is the way my family lived before the Egyptians came." It had been a long time since Ramose had heard her laugh so much.

The nomads were strange-looking people. There were three dark men, all like the one who had leaned over him, all wearing long-sleeved, hairy coats that came down to their ankles. They had pieces of dark cloth wrapped around their heads.

There were also five women and some children. The women had patterns tattooed in dark blue on their faces. They wore heavy beaded necklaces and bracelets. They had rings, not on their fingers, but pierced through their ears and noses. The children were tending a herd of about twenty goats, giving them dry grass from a sack.

It was the strangest sight Ramose had ever seen, but strangest of all was the camel creature. It carried leather saddlebags and rolls of cloth. Large terracotta jars and metal cooking pots hung on either side of the animal's strange humped back.

Ramose realised it was the animal's strong smell that he had smelt as he was pulled behind it. The strange sounds he'd heard were the jars and pots knocking against each other.

Ramose watched as the people made their camp in the desert. They stuck sticks into the sand and draped heavy cloth over them, holding down the edges with stones. In less than an hour there was a comfortable little village: four cloth houses and a cooking fire.

"Don't they want to know who we are, what we're doing?" asked Ramose.

"No. Desert people welcome all travellers." Karoya's eyes shone. "Anyone who comes to their camp is made welcome and given food."

Ramose thought that the children would have been more interested in their strange guests, but they were all huddled around something, laughing and squealing. One of them stood up with the object of their fascination in his arms. It was Mery.

"They have never seen a cat before," Karoya said. "They had never even heard of such a creature."

One little girl, who was no more than four, reached out slowly to the cat. She touched the fur and Mery miaowed. The little girl jumped back in terror. Ramose found it hard to believe that the children could be frightened of a little cat, yet they played happily at the feet of the monster animal they called camel.

"I have never heard of camels," said Ramose.

"It is from a far distant place where there are

many such creatures," Karoya explained. "Zeyd won the creature in a fight with the chief of an enemy tribe. The camel doesn't need to drink like other animals. Zeyd believes that it stores water in the hump on its back. He wishes that he had more camels."

"I thought you said you didn't speak their language."

"I don't. Zeyd explained with his voice and his hands and pictures in the sand."

Ramose inspected his leg, which was bandaged in coarse cloth and squashed under a heavy stone. He lifted off the stone and unwrapped his leg.

"The weight of the stone stopped the poison from spreading to other parts of your body," Karoya explained.

Large leaves were pressed into the area where he'd been bitten. Ramose gently removed them.

"These look like lotus leaves," he said.

"They are. They stop the pain. The leaves are very precious to desert people because they are hard to get. The lotus plant is very useful. There was some powdered lotus in the milk you drank as well."

Ramose's lower leg was still swollen and there were two puncture marks in his calf.

"The poison in desert scorpions is strong and you were bitten twice. If the nomads had not appeared out of the desert," Karoya said quietly, "I think you would have died."

The nomad women lit a small fire using dried palm fronds and dung just as Karoya did. Hapu helped Ramose to his feet and led him to the fire. There was the smell of roasting goat's meat and baking bread. Ramose's stomach growled. It had been weeks since he'd eaten properly.

As soon as the sun dropped below the horizon, it got cold, colder than Ramose had ever known it to be in Egypt. He shivered, even though he was sitting as close as possible to the flames.

Zeyd, the man he had seen earlier, said something to one of the women. She disappeared inside a tent and returned with warm clothes for the guests. Ramose gratefully pulled on a long, hairy garment similar to the other men's—a dark, heavy coat that reached the ground. From the smell of it, Ramose guessed it was made of woven goat hair. He was getting used to the strong smell of goats already, and it was good to feel warm.

They all sat around the fire and ate a meal of goat's meat, bread and a vegetable that Ramose didn't recognise. After that there were dates and warm milk. The nomads talked among themselves in their strange language. The children stared at Mery who was curled up in Karoya's lap. They giggled as Hapu pulled faces and did little tricks for them.

"I can't believe they don't want to know who we are," Ramose said.

"They think that is our business, not theirs," said Karoya.

"How do they know we're not planning to steal their goats?" asked Hapu.

"It doesn't matter. It would be a shameful thing to turn away a traveller in the desert, even if he's an enemy."

"We're not their enemies though," said Ramose.

"Yes, we are," said Karoya. "At least you two are. Egyptians are the enemies of all desert people. They kill them for no reason or enslave them. You especially are their enemy, Ramose."

"Would it make a difference if they knew who I was?"

"No, even the pharaoh's son would be welcome."

Ramose looked around at the nomads. The men were discussing their goats. The women were clearing away the remains of the meal and mending clothes and tents. The children were getting sleepy. The younger ones were already asleep in their mothers' laps.

"How can I thank Zeyd?" Ramose asked Karoya.

"You don't have to," she replied. "He expects that you would do the same for him."

Like most Egyptians, Ramose had never met any barbarians before. He had never imagined that he would one day be accepting their hospitality, enjoying their food and sleeping in their tents.

Ramose offered to sleep outside, but Zeyd refused. Ramose slept a dreamless sleep, more peaceful than any since he had left the Great Place.

They spent the next two days travelling through the desert, seeing nothing but sand. Each morning the tents were taken down, the camel was loaded up and the nomads walked through the desert, herding the goats in front of them. They left behind them nothing but their footsteps and the tent stones, piled together for other nomads to use.

Ramose sat on the sled at first, but by the second day he was able to walk for part of the day. The children took it in turns to carry Mery's basket. Even the smallest insisted on carrying it for a few paces.

The sand stretched out before them flat in all directions. It was hard and, as they walked, their feet made a hollow, booming sound as if they were walking across the stretched skin of a drum. The sun burned down on them and turned the yellow sand to a glaring white.

"I can see water ahead," said Hapu as they walked. "Look, there's a lake!"

Karoya laughed at him. "It's not a lake. It's the sun playing tricks on your eyes."

Ramose could see the shimmering mirage as well, a pool of reflected sky just ahead of them.

"My people call it the devil's mirror," said Karoya.

Ramose shaded his eyes to look at the mirage. They kept walking towards it, but they never got any closer. It was always just ahead of them.

After two days of seeing nothing but flat sand stretching in every direction, two dark dots appeared in the distance.

"Is that another mirage?" asked Hapu.

Karoya shook her head.

As they drew closer, Ramose could see that it was two piles of rocks. Zeyd smiled and nodded when they reached them. The women replaced rocks that the wind had blown from the piles. Then they swept away sand that had built up against them.

"They are signposts," said Karoya. "It means that we are heading in the right direction. The piles of stones are a gateway leading to the road ahead."

Hapu walked between the two piles and looked around him. There was still nothing but sand.

"It looks like a gateway to nowhere," he said.

The nomads laughed at Hapu, even though they couldn't understand what he said.

3

GATEWAY TO NOWHERE

O N THE THIRD DAY, the landscape changed. The sand gradually started to rise and fall. Then it piled up into dunes. The dunes grew bigger and bigger until they were towering above them on either side. The colour of the sand changed too, from yellow to pink to pale purple.

"I didn't realise that sand could be so many

different shapes and colours," Ramose said to Karoya as they walked.

"I told you the desert was beautiful," said Karoya. "You didn't believe me."

"I still wouldn't call it beautiful, but I'm starting to see it a little differently."

Ramose didn't feel threatened by the desert as he had when he first left the Nile Valley. He still couldn't imagine living in it permanently, but it didn't hold the same fears for him as before.

"Do you have any idea where we're going, though?" asked Hapu, joining them as they walked.

"We're walking south, that's all I know," said Ramose, looking up at the sun.

"Eventually we'll have to stop going south and find the river again," said Hapu.

At midday, the nomads stopped for a short while to drink milk and eat bread. Then they continued their journey. Hapu was getting bored.

"Let's play a game," he said enthusiastically.

"If we stop to play, we'll get left behind," said Ramose.

"I was thinking of a game we could play while we're walking," said Hapu. "I'll think of something that we can all see. I'll tell you what sound it begins with and you have to guess what it is."

"It'll be a short game. All we can see is sand!"

"Try it and see," said Hapu. "It'll be fun."

Ramose and Karoya agreed to play the game. Hapu was very inventive and thought of things like sand grain, camel tail and goat's ear. Even so, it didn't take long until they had used every possible thing that they could see. Ramose, whose body was still healing from the effects of the scorpion poison, was happy just to walk and let his mind wander.

His body was still weak, but inside Ramose felt strong. The fact that he had survived the scorpion bite gave him courage. Vizier Wersu had attacked him and he'd survived. He knew that the vizier had only been a vision, that it was really the scorpion that had nearly killed him, but in his mind he felt as if he'd overcome his enemy. He didn't know where the nomads were going, but he knew he was getting closer to Thebes. Every step was taking him closer to his home and his family.

In the afternoon, a breeze picked up. Grains of sand blew gently across the surface of the dunes.

"I'd forgotten what a breeze was like," said Ramose, turning his face towards the faint rush of cooler air.

The nomads didn't seem pleased about the breeze and made the camel walk faster.

The breeze became a wind. The sand started to shift slightly. The wind blew the sides of the dunes into steeper and steeper slopes until they eventually collapsed and cascaded into new shapes. The wind grew stronger and the blowing sand started to sting their hands and faces. The nomads unwound the cloth from their heads and covered their faces with it. The long nomad coats protected the friends' arms and legs. Ramose and Hapu had nothing to shield their faces from the sharp sand. Karoya wrapped her striped cloth over her face. She also took Mery's basket from the children and held it close to her, muttering reassuring words to the cat.

Within an hour, the wind was howling and they had to bend over almost double to protect themselves from the fierce stream of stinging sand. The wind howled and roared like some sort of wild beast. Ramose couldn't see any more than a cubit in front of him.

"Why don't we stop and wait for the wind to die down?" he shouted to Karoya.

"It's too dangerous," she yelled back. "If you sit still in a sandstorm, the sand will bury you. We have to keep moving. Just stay behind the camel."

Ramose shouted to Hapu. "Stay close." He grabbed his friends' hands and they bent into the wind.

Ramose lost all sense of time. He couldn't tell whether the sandstorm had been blowing for a

few minutes or for hours. He hung on tightly to
Hapu and Karoya's hands. Every now and again
he glanced up to make sure that he could still see
the camel's rump in front of him.

Suddenly, Karoya's hand was wrenched out of
his. He turned. Through the stream of flying sand
he saw that her legs had disappeared up to her
knees.

"It's a sand pool," she yelled. Her voice was
almost lost in the roar and screech of the wind.
"Soft sand. I'm sinking."

Ramose stumbled towards her.

"No! Don't come closer or you'll sink too,"
Karoya shouted. "Get Mery!"

The cat's basket was sitting on top of the soft
sand, too light to sink. Ramose reached out and
grabbed it. Karoya was sinking further into the
sand. In a few moments she would disappear
completely.

Ramose quickly took off the long garment that
he was wearing and, holding on to one end, threw
the other end to Karoya. She reached out for it,
but couldn't grab hold. The sharp sand bit into
Ramose's bare skin. It felt like a thousand scorpions were stinging him.

"Hapu," he shouted. "Hold on to my hand."

He could hardly see Karoya now. She was
struggling to clamber out of the soft sand, but the
more she struggled the further she sank into it.

With Hapu clinging onto his hand, Ramose edged towards the sand pool. He could feel his feet sink up to his ankles. He didn't dare go any further. He threw the coat towards Karoya again. She managed to grab hold of one of the sleeves. Ramose felt his legs disappear into the sand.

"Pull me back," he screamed at Hapu. "I'm sinking too."

He felt his friend grip him around the waist with both hands. Ramose held on to the hem of his coat. He felt the cloth give slightly and realised with horror that the stitching in the sleeve was breaking. He leaned out further, amazed that skinny little Hapu had found the strength to hold the weight of both Karoya and him. He hoped he could keep it up.

Ramose hauled in the garment hand over hand. The stitches kept breaking, until the sleeve was only attached to a couple of finger-widths of cloth. Ramose reached out and grasped hold of the sleeve just as the last stitch broke. He pulled the sleeve with all his might until he could see Karoya's fingers about to lose their grip. He grabbed her by the wrist. Once she felt him, she reached out with her other hand and grabbed hold of his arm with a grip like crocodile jaws. Ramose's strength was fading, but he knew he couldn't let his friend go. Using his arm like a rope, Karoya clawed her way to the edge of the sand pool and crawled back to firmer ground. All three collapsed exhausted onto the sand.

After a while the wind started to die down. The biting sand stopped blowing at them. The air finally cleared. They looked around.

"Where are the nomads?" said Hapu.

Ramose, worn out after so much exertion so soon after his sickness, didn't have the strength to move. Karoya struggled to the top of a dune. She turned in a circle, scanning the horizon in all directions.

"I can't see them anywhere."

Ramose crawled up the sand dune. He had to see for himself. Huge dunes stretched in every direction like a sheet of crumpled papyrus. He strained his eyes looking for a series of black shapes that would represent the nomads and their animals. All he could see was sand.

"They have to be out there somewhere," he said. "There hasn't been enough time for them to walk over the horizon."

"They're hidden by the dunes. Even if we did wait here until we caught sight of them, we wouldn't be able to catch up with them."

The sun was low in the sky. They were all dead tired after their ordeal. Ramose and Karoya crawled back down the dune and collapsed.

As the darkness crept around them, the three friends huddled together. Ramose closed his eyes.

He saw an image of the desert, nothing but sand in every direction as far as the eye could see. On the endless sand he could see three small black dots. That was them. They were lost, hopelessly lost. They had no food, and hardly any water. Ramose could think of nothing on earth that could save them. He prayed to Seth, who was also the god of the desert and foreign lands, not to abandon him and his friends.

"We could last for quite a while without food," Karoya said, as they sat in the growing light the following morning. "But without water, we haven't got a chance."

She shook their water-skin. It was less than a quarter full.

"Zeyd will come back and look for us, won't he?" Hapu asked hopefully.

Karoya stroked Mery and shook her head.

"He helped us before."

"He didn't change the path of his journey, though. Nomads have to keep moving to the next oasis. They couldn't risk the lives of their goats by stopping to look for us. Without the goats the nomads die."

They sat in silence as the sun rose in the sky.

Ramose sat up. He still felt very weak. "We should walk east, towards the Nile."

"The river must be many days march away,"

said Karoya. "We can't possibly reach it without food or water."

"I'd rather walk than sit and wait for death."

"Okay. We'll walk," said Hapu.

Karoya nodded. She sewed the sleeve back onto Ramose's nomad coat as best she could with a length of fishing line.

"I'm sorry," Ramose said. "Neither of you would be in this situation if it wasn't for me."

Ramose looked at his friends. Why had they chosen to take this journey with him? It was the duty of all Egyptians to serve the pharaoh and his family, but when Hapu started to help Ramose, he didn't even know he was the pharaoh's son. Karoya should have hated him. It was the pharaoh who was responsible for her being taken from her family and becoming a slave.

"You shouldn't have followed me, Hapu."

Hapu put his bag on his shoulder. "It's the will of the gods," he said.

"You could have gone to Tombos, Karoya. You would have been closer to your home. Why did you choose to come with me?"

Karoya shrugged. "You needed my help."

Ramose had hoped that when he became pharaoh, he would be able to reward his friends for their friendship. It didn't look like that was going to happen now.

Ramose turned towards the rising sun and

started to walk. Hapu followed him. Karoya picked up Mery's basket and set out after Hapu.

No one spoke. There was nothing to say. The sun beat down on them. It felt hotter than it had on the other days they'd spent in the desert. By mid-morning they had already drunk all the water. Ramose could think of nothing but how thirsty he was. He imagined large terracotta jars of water, pools and ponds; he remembered the Nile. He didn't look ahead, but just stared at the sand beneath him, and his feet making one point-less step after another. They trudged through the valleys between the huge mounds of sand, skirt-ing around dune after dune.

"Ramose," said Karoya behind him. Her voice sounded dry and crackly like a piece of burnt papyrus. "You've turned south. We aren't heading east any more."

Ramose looked up at the sun. It was directly above them. When the sun was in that position he found it hard to tell which way was which.

"What does it matter?" he said, continuing to walk in the same direction.

Karoya didn't argue. She followed in his foot-steps. Hapu's eyes were glazed over. Ramose had seen that look in animals that were close to death. He guessed his own eyes had the same look. Ramose kept walking.

The visions of water in Ramose's head grew

stronger. He remembered the jars and jars of water that the palace servants had poured over him day after day as they bathed him. He also remembered the lotus pool in the palace gardens. He pictured the irrigation canals in the Nile valley, recalling with envy the water poured on the rows of vegetables. He would have given anything for a cup of water, just the amount given to a single lettuce or onion plant. But he had nothing to give.

Images of his dear sister and Keneben, his tutor, drifted into his mind. The last time he had seen them was the day they had escaped from the high priest. The royal barge had sailed past them on its way to Thebes. Aboard it, Ramose had seen his beautiful sister, Princess Hatshepsut, and Keneben. He had thought Keneben was still banished in the distant land of Punt.

Ramose had also glimpsed his father on the barge. Pharaoh had looked unwell, but he was healthy enough to make the long river journey to Thebes. Ramose had splashed into the river waving and shouting, but they hadn't seen him. They didn't know where he was. They would never know what had happened to him. He had also seen his half-brother, the brat Prince Tuthmosis, and the boy's evil mother Queen Mutnofret.

When darkness fell, they collapsed in the sand.

When the sun rose, they struggled to their feet and walked again. They walked without thinking about which direction they were going in. They each stared down at their feet, as if a great deal of concentration was required to keep them moving. Their steps became slower and shorter, until they were merely shuffling through the sand a few finger-widths at a time.

Ramose looked up at the sky. The sun was lower. Was it morning or afternoon? He couldn't remember. Was this only the second day of walking? Surely it had been longer. He looked around him. The dunes had softened and become smaller and lower. Instead of walking around them, they walked in a straight line over them. It was easier than having to decide which valley to follow. Ramose stopped. Up ahead he saw something glint in the sunlight. It was a reflection of the blue sky.

"The devil's mirror," said Ramose hoarsely, pointing to the reflection.

Karoya looked to where he was pointing. She nodded. Her knees collapsed beneath her, as if the effort of nodding had taken all the energy she had. She slumped to the ground. Hapu collapsed next to her. Ramose kept his eyes on the bright glint of reflected light. This mirage was more detailed than the ones he'd seen before. He could actually see faint images of palm fronds. Ramose thought it must be the effects of lack of water. He stumbled a few more steps. The reflection disappeared, but the image of the palm tree grew clearer.

"I must be close to death," he whispered, though the words couldn't get out of his parched mouth. "I'm seeing things."

He shuffled up the gentle slope of the next sand dune, but his legs crumpled beneath him. He crawled on his hands and knees, as the palm fronds in front of him multiplied and tamarisks appeared as well. Suddenly, the sand beneath him sprouted tufts of dry grass. He crawled to the top of the dune. A green valley stretched before him. A forest of date palms, tamarisks and acacia trees sprung from the ground. In the middle of the trees was a pool of water, perfectly reflecting the sky. Ramose stared.

He croaked out a call to his friends. They struggled to their feet and made their way very slowly to the top of the shallow dune. They blinked as they stared at the brilliant vision of green and blue—colours they hadn't seen for days and days.

"Is it real?" Hapu's voice was a hoarse whisper, "or have we passed into the underworld?"

Ramose stood up and took a few steps towards the trees and the pool. They didn't edge further away as he approached, as the heat haze had.

Instead they grew closer. He could see that the palms were laden with dates. Ramose found a last reserve of energy and ran towards the pool. He splashed into the water and then fell full length. The coolness of the water took his breath away. He gulped in mouthfuls of it.

"It's real," he spluttered.

4

ORACLE OF
THE OASIS

AROYA AND HAPU approached the pool more cautiously. Karoya dipped her fingers into the water and scooped up a handful. She drank it and then sank to her knees to drink more. Hapu stood ankle-deep in the water and cried.

"I don't understand how there can be a pool of water in the middle of the desert," Hapu said, after they had drunk their fill. The water had a bitter, salty taste, but no one was complaining. They were sitting in the shade of a tamarisk tree chewing on the dried-up dates that had fallen on the ground. No one had the strength yet to climb one of the palms for the fresher fruit.

"It's an oasis," said Ramose.

"Without them nomads wouldn't be able to survive," said Karoya.

"But where does the water come from?" asked Hapu, still puzzled.

"It comes up from the great invisible river that runs beneath the earth," replied Karoya.

Hapu shook his head in disbelief. "It's like magic."

Ramose didn't want to spoil his friends' good mood, but he was already thinking of what lay ahead of them.

"The Nile is still many, many cubits away and we only have one small water-skin and nothing but dates to eat."

"We can live here for a long time," said Karoya. "There will be snakes, birds, frogs. We can find things to eat."

"And stay here until we grow old?" Hapu didn't like the idea.

"No," replied Karoya. "We will wait until the next nomads arrive."

"That could be ages."

"It might be months, yes. Do you have a better idea?"

Hapu didn't.

The sun was low in the sky.

"It will be getting cold soon," said Karoya. "We need to collect fuel to make a fire."

The three friends walked around the oasis collecting dead palm fronds and dry grass.

"Look what I've found," shouted Karoya. She picked up a dead branch that had fallen from one of the tamarisk trees. "We'll be able to have a good fire tonight."

Wood was very precious in Egypt and they wouldn't have dreamt of wasting it in a fire normally, but out in the desert it didn't seem to matter.

Karoya arranged some stones to make a fireplace. She laid a pile of grass and palm leaves in the fireplace and then she got out her fire-making tools. These consisted of three pieces of wood: a flat stick with a well dug into it, a smooth rod and a stick with a length of gut tied at each end like a small bow. She wrapped the string of the bow around the rod and placed the end of the rod in the well in the flat stick. Then she started pulling the bow back and forth so that the upright stick twirled at great speed. Hapu laid small pieces of dry grass near the well, waiting for the wood to get hot enough to burn the grass. Ramose picked up the dead tree branch and broke it across his knee. The crack echoed in the silence. A shrill sound suddenly came out of the trees.

"Eigh! Eigh! Eigh!"

The friends all spun round. Hapu screamed in terror. A small dark creature, covered from head to toe in black rags, appeared from among the trees. It was wielding a heavy stick. The creature ran straight at Ramose, knocked him to the ground and started hitting him with the stick.

"It's a demon," yelled Hapu.

Karoya rushed at the demon, trying to rescue her friend.

"Stop!" she shouted.

The creature turned with a whirl of tattered rags and set upon Karoya, scratching her with long, curved claws and growling like a tiger. Ramose jumped to his feet and grabbed the demon, pinning its arms behind its back. He was surprised at how easy it was. The creature's arms were thin and frail. He pulled back the black rags wrapped around its head to get a better look at their attacker. To his surprise, he discovered it was an old woman—an ancient woman. She had a tangle of grey hair, milky-white eyes and a dark-brown face that was wrinkled like an old leather bag. She screamed out horrible sounds and feebly tried to escape from Ramose's grasp.

"It must be the spirit of someone who died in

the desert?" said Hapu, looking at her fearfully.

"I don't think spirits can bash people," said Ramose, rubbing the bump on his head.

"Where did she come from?" asked Karoya, peering around in the growing darkness. "There's no one else here."

"Where are your people?" Ramose asked the old woman. "Where are you from?"

The woman didn't seem to understand him. Hapu waved his hand in front of her eyes.

"I think she's blind," he said.

"I'll keep an eye on her," said Ramose. "You two see if you can find something to eat."

Since their last meal with the nomads two days before, they'd had nothing to eat but a few dried dates.

"Hapu, can you climb up one of these palms and get some dates?"

Hapu nodded and started to climb a date palm.

"Dates," said the old woman in an angry voice. "My dates."

The three friends stared at the wrinkled face. She had spoken in Egyptian.

"We're hungry," said Karoya slowly. "Very hungry."

The old woman's brow wrinkled even more than it was already. She reached up and touched Karoya's face.

"Children!" she exclaimed. She spoke with a

heavy accent, and the word came slowly as if she was searching in a part of her mind she hadn't used for a long time. "Come!" she said. "Come!"

The woman led Karoya by the hand. It was almost dark now, but the old woman walked confidently through the trees as if it were broad daylight. Ramose and Hapu looked at each other, and then followed her.

"I thought she was blind," whispered Hapu.

"She is, but she must know the oasis very well."

The woman led them away from the pool and through the grove of trees to a rocky outcrop. There was a fireplace with a fire smouldering in it. A piece of dark material, similar to the nomads' tents, hung from a rock overhang. It was held in place by stones. The woman must have slept behind this rough curtain. There were cooking pots and baskets. Tethered nearby were three goats.

"It looks like she's lived here for a long time," said Ramose.

The woman made them sit down. There was a cooking pot on the fire. Something was simmering inside it—something that smelled like meat cooking. Such delicious smells had seemed unimaginable half an hour ago. The woman made bread from flour. She gave them each a gourd bowl and filled them to the brim with the goat stew. They ate ravenously.

"It tastes wonderful," said Hapu, gratefully.

While they were eating, the old woman made sweet cakes with honey and dates. They ate them, still hot, with fresh goats' milk. It was a feast.

"I think this is all a mirage," said Ramose, swallowing another cake. "Like the heat haze pools we saw out in the desert."

"Yes, but we couldn't get near them," said Hapu, draining his bowl of milk. "This isn't moving away."

An angry miaow came from Karoya's basket. Karoya leapt up to open it.

"I forgot about Mery!" she said, letting the cat out. "Poor Mery, you're hungry too, aren't you?"

Mery wailed miserably. The old woman jumped at the sound. Karoya put down her bowl of milk and let the cat drink. Mery purred. The old woman was puzzled by the sound. She cocked her ear to listen more closely.

"It's a cat," Karoya replied. "It's my pet."

The old woman had heard of cats, but thought they were imaginary beasts like griffins and camels. Ramose smiled to himself, remembering the camel. Karoya guided the woman's hand so that it stroked Mery's fur. The old woman's grim little mouth broke into a smile.

"Warm," she said. "Soft."

Now that the friends had eaten their fill and

were warmed by the fire, they began to relax. The old woman, speaking slowly in a half-forgotten language, told them her story.

They discovered that her name was Jenu. When she was a young girl, her father had been the chief of a nomad tribe, just like the one they had travelled with.

"One day we went to Kharga, an oasis so big it takes a week to walk from one end to the other," she told them. "Egyptians were there, building their temples. They took away all the young people for slaves." Jenu shook her head sorrowfully. "I lived for many years as a slave in the house of an Egyptian."

When her eyesight started to fail, her master didn't want to feed a blind slave. She was taken to the edge of the desert and left there; told to return to her tribe. Of course, she had no idea where her people would be. She wandered for many days and was close to death when a tribe of nomads came across her. It had been a bad year in the desert and the nomads had lost many of their goats. They could not take on another mouth to feed. Instead, they brought her to the oasis, gave her some food and left her there when they moved on. If the gods will it, you will survive, they had said.

"And the gods did will it," said the old woman. "May they be praised forever."

After the food ran out, Jenu had lived on dates and frogs. Then other nomads came to the oasis and each tribe gave her a little of what they had.

"I give them something in return," said Jenu.

"What?" asked Ramose. "What do you have to give?"

She told them how, as her vision of the world had disappeared, she had discovered an inner vision was growing in its place.

"The gods, in their wisdom, have made me an oracle," she said. "I can read people's futures."

Stories of the Oracle of the Oasis had spread among the nomads. Now, whenever they visited the oasis, they asked Jenu to look into their future.

Ramose and his friends sat wide-eyed listening to Jenu's story, forgetting their exhaustion.

"Can you see everyone's future?" asked Hapu.

Jenu shook her head. "Only those who the gods favour." She reached out and found Ramose's hand. "She will lift the mists on your future."

The old woman wouldn't say anything else and disappeared into her tent, telling them she was tired.

The following morning the friends awoke to find Jenu making breakfast. After they had eaten fresh bread, goats' cheese and dried figs, they explored the oasis. It was quite small, perhaps a thousand cubits from one end to the other. Ramose remembered courtyards in the palace that were bigger.

As well as the tethered goats, Jenu had a small garden where she grew a patch of wheat, some herbs and onions. Other food, gifts from nomads, was stored in jars and baskets. Nomads had been there only two weeks earlier, so her stores were full.

Jenu had a list of things that she wanted her visitors to do for her. Her simple weaving loom had broken and she wanted them to mend it for her. She wanted someone to climb the trees and knock down fresh dates. The sharp-edged stone that she used for cutting had shattered and she needed a new one.

The oasis was a pleasant place. Karoya and Hapu spent the whole day helping the old woman. Mery skipped around, attacking tufts of grass and chasing birds, delighted that she was no longer squashed in her basket. Jenu was enjoying the company of her young guests. She no longer looked like a frightening old witch. Overnight she had transformed into a smiling grandmother.

Ramose busied himself around the oasis, but he wasn't laughing and chattering like the others. He was thinking about what the old woman had said the night before. Could she really see into his future? If she could, did he want to know what she saw?

In the evening, after a filling meal of tasty goat stew, Karoya and Hapu sat around Jenu's cooking fire as if they hadn't a problem in the world. Jenu sat spinning goat hair into thread, twirling it with her fingers. Hapu told funny stories that made the old woman laugh. Karoya mended Jenu's tattered tent cloth. Mery lay with her stomach towards the fire. Ramose sat to one side, poking at the fire. He knew that his problems weren't over yet.

"Jenu, do you know how far it is to the river?" he asked.

The others fell silent.

"A long way," said the old woman.

"How many days on foot?" Ramose asked.

"Many days," replied the old woman.

Ramose could tell she was being unhelpful on purpose. He knew he had to ask her the question he had been avoiding. He poked at the embers of the fire, sending out sparks that singed Mery's fur and made her leap up. The cat settled down again, this time in Jenu's lap. Mery had grown fond of the old woman who gave her milk and meat.

"Jenu," said Ramose at last. "Can you see my future?"

She beckoned Ramose. He got up and sat next

to the old woman. She took his hand in hers. He could feel the calluses on her palms. Her long, claw-like fingernails scraped his skin. Her face changed. The smiling grandmother face disappeared and was replaced by a stern-faced mask. Jenu's white unseeing eyes changed too. They lost their sightless look and Ramose felt as if she could see right into his soul. A single gust of wind arose out of the perfectly still night. A distant hyena chose that moment to howl.

"Some things I see. Others are unclear."

"Tell me what you see."

"You must give me something first. Something dear to you."

Ramose reached for his bag. He only had one thing to give. He pulled out his heart scarab, stroked its cool surface and put the blue jewel in Jenu's hand.

The old woman felt the stone with her crooked fingers and shook her head.

"Not this," she said. "I have no need of this."

"But it's the only thing of value I have," Ramose said.

"You have to give something that I need," replied the old woman.

"You seem to have all you need. I have nothing else to give you."

The old woman's white eyes narrowed. "You have friendship."

"If you want my friendship, you have it already," said Ramose.

The old woman shook her head. "But you will leave and I will only have the memory of friendship."

"Are you saying you want me to stay?" asked Ramose.

"Not you. You have a journey to finish. You have friends. I have no one."

Ramose looked at Karoya and Hapu in alarm, finally understanding what the old woman wanted. They were staring back at him wide-eyed.

"I can't give you my friends," said Ramose. "They aren't mine to give."

"The slave girl is yours to give, if you choose."

"No," Ramose cried, his voice rising in fear and anger. "I don't own her. She's free to go wherever she wishes."

"Is she?"

Ramose knew that Karoya was actually the pharaoh's property.

"She is useful to you now," continued Jenu. "But if you find what you are seeking, then what will become of her?"

"I'll take care of her." Ramose snatched his hand away. "I've changed my mind. I don't want to know my future."

"The choice is yours," said Jenu.

"Why can't you just tell him?" asked Hapu.

"It is the way of the oracle. She will not see clearly unless Ramose gives me something of his that I need."

Mery stirred in the old woman's lap. The cat stood up, turned around twice then settled down again.

"What about Mery?" asked Karoya.

"No, Karoya," said Ramose. "Mery is yours. Jenu wants something of mine."

Karoya turned to the old woman. "Would the cat be a suitable gift?" she asked. "She is a good friend."

The old woman thought for a moment and then nodded.

"I don't want to hear about my future," said Ramose angrily. "I don't believe in oracles. I know what I have to do. I don't need an oracle to tell me."

"The oracle's knowledge is important," said the old woman. "Without it you might fail."

"I give Mery to you, Ramose," said Karoya. Mery slept in the old woman's lap, unaware that she was the centre of attention. "She is yours now."

"No!"

"The gods have brought us here, Ramose," said Hapu. "Perhaps it was for a reason. Listen to what Jenu has to say."

"Let her tell your future instead," Ramose said. "Or yours, Karoya."

"No, Ramose," said Karoya. "My future has been bound with yours since I chose to follow you and not go where the pharaoh sent me. Take Mery. I give her to you."

Ramose looked from Karoya to the old woman.

"Are you sure, Karoya?"

"I'm sure."

"Will you give the cat to me, Ramose?" asked the old woman.

Ramose nodded. "Yes."

"The oracle accepts your gift," said Jenu. She spoke as if the oracle was another person.

The old woman reached out for Ramose's hand again. Ramose glared at the old woman, but placed his hand in hers.

"Ask the oracle what you want to know."

There was so much he wanted to know, Ramose hardly knew where to begin. "Will I see my father again before he dies?"

"Yes."

"Will I achieve my goal?"

"Yes."

"Will I—"

"You can ask only one more question of the oracle."

"Why didn't you say that before?" snapped Ramose. "This isn't a game."

"The oracle doesn't like to give up her knowledge."

Ramose had so many questions. If he were to become the pharaoh, would he be happy? Would he be a good pharaoh? Would Vizier Wersu still want him dead? Ramose thought for a moment. He had to word his last question carefully.

"Does the oracle see anything in my future that I need to know?"

The old woman smiled a small, grim smile. "The oracle has a warning for you."

"What is it?"

"The blue lotus can hide a bee in its petals."

Ramose opened his mouth to say something. The old woman held up her hand to stop him.

"A perfect jewel will stay buried in the earth, yet the maid at the millstone holds it out in her hand."

Jenu still held her hand in the air.

"Trust the crocodile and bow down before the frog."

Ramose waited, expecting more. But the hard mask of the old woman's face melted away and she changed back into a smiling grandmother again.

"Is that it?" Ramose cried.

Jenu nodded. "The oracle's words are truth." She looked limp and drained.

"But, they're just riddles. What do they mean?"

"That's for you to discover. The oracle has been generous. She doesn't often say so much."

Ramose felt cheated, as if the old woman had tricked him. He took his reed mat and unrolled it away from the others. He curled up in the smelly goat-hair coat that the nomads had given him. He didn't want to speak to anybody.

5

ABYDOS

T HE NEXT DAY, Ramose woke with a sense of urgency. He had dreamt he'd seen his father walking in the palace gardens. In the dream Ramose had called out to him, but Pharaoh couldn't hear him. Ramose had tried to get closer to him, but whichever way he turned there was a wall or a pond or a row of tall plants in his way. Ramose knew he had to leave the oasis. He had delayed for too long. "I'm walking to Thebes," he told his friends. "I have to leave immediately."

"You don't know how far it is to the river," said Karoya. "You may not be able to carry enough food and water to get you there.'

"It's too risky," complained Hapu.

"I have to go," said Ramose. "You two stay here and wait for the next nomads to come along."

Ramose didn't like to admit it, but the oracle's words had affected him strongly. He still didn't know what they meant, but whatever his destiny was, he had to face it. He had wandered from his path. He had wasted valuable time. He had to get to Thebes as soon as possible. He had to see his father.

He asked Jenu if he could have some leather for a water-skin. She nodded and cut him a length of goat hide from her stock. She showed him how to make the bag with the hairy side facing in. She also gave him a supply of dried goat meat and cheese. Ramose mended his sandals and his nomad coat. By the time he had finished his preparations, it was too late in the day to start his journey.

"We're not staying behind," said Karoya as the sun started to get low in the sky. "We're coming with you."

"You don't have to," said Ramose. "Stay here."

"And then what would we do?" asked Hapu.

Ramose looked at his friends. Since the day they had chosen to follow him instead of going to the place that had been allotted to them, their destinies were tied up with his.

Hapu looked at the pool of water unhappily. "I think it would be better if we all waited here until other nomads come. But if you want to leave now, I'll come too."

"I'll be grateful for your company."

They left before sunrise the next morning. Jenu bade them all goodbye.

"The gods will be with you," said the old woman. "They won't abandon you."

Karoya said goodbye to Mery with tears in her eyes. Jenu clutched Mery to her in case she tried to follow them.

"The cat will keep me warm at night," Jenu said happily.

Earlier, Ramose had offered to come back and give her as much gold as she wanted once he had achieved his goal, if she gave the cat back. The old woman had refused.

The three friends loaded themselves up with food and water and walked out into the desert. The sun rose in front of them. They walked towards it in single file, keeping space between them. No one felt like talking.

In the heat of midday, they stopped and made a shelter from the hot sun with a length of goat-hair cloth and some sticks that Jenu had given them. They ate a light meal, drank a little water and slept until the worst of the heat had passed.

When they woke, they walked until two or three hours after the sun had set, then ate cold meat and cheese. They slept again and then walked in the darkness before dawn. They spoke little, not wanting to waste precious energy on idle talk.

Ramose wasn't sure that they would make it to the river. He wasn't convinced that he had a future just because a blind nomad woman had told him so. He kept walking.

Ramose glanced at Karoya. She had hardly spoken since they had left the oasis. Once or twice he had seen her wipe away some tears. He knew what a great sacrifice she had made for him. Karoya loved Mery dearly. The cat had been the only thing that was truly hers and she had given it away for his sake. All he'd got in return for her sacrifice were a few meaningless words from the oracle. He hoped one day he'd be able to repay her.

The routine was the same the next day and the next. Ramose didn't tire; he just grew stronger and stronger. He began to feel like the desert would never stop and that didn't matter because

he knew he could walk forever. He was very surprised, therefore, when at mid-morning on the
fifth day a large temple gradually rose up over
the horizon, bright and shimmering in the heat
haze. He recognised it immediately. It was a
place he had visited before.

Abydos was a big town, not as big as Thebes,
but big nonetheless. It had sprung up around the
Temple of Osiris. The people who lived in the
town all worked at the temple. Those who didn't
have jobs within the temple buildings worked
outside the walls producing food for the workers
and for offerings to Osiris.

"We shouldn't have come into the town," hissed
Karoya.

"We had to. We've run out of food."

Ramose hoped that in such a big town they
might not attract as much attention as they had
in the villages along the Nile. He was wrong. He
hadn't realised how foreign they looked. They
were still wearing the heavy clothing made from
dark, hairy cloth given to them by the nomads.
They hadn't bathed properly in weeks. Ramose
had no idea what his hair looked like, but Hapu's
was a tangled mess.

The temple workers in their white linen kilts
and tunics looked spotlessly clean. They all
smelled of perfumed oils and incense. Everyone
who passed Ramose and his friends stepped

around them so that they didn't get too close to the foul-smelling foreigners.

"What are we going to do?" said Ramose. "We have no gold for food. We can't beg on the streets."

They wandered through Abydos, past the neat houses of the temple workers. Wherever they went, people turned to stare at them. They walked through the metalworkers' quarter. The sound of hammers and bellows stopped as they passed. It was the same as they walked through the part of the town where the potters worked. The potters' wheels stopped turning and all eyes followed the strangers.

"We'll get arrested," said Hapu.

"What for? We haven't done anything wrong," said Ramose.

"Not recently," said Hapu.

"Egyptians don't like strangers," said Karoya. "People will want to know who we are. What are you going to tell them?"

"I'll think of something," Ramose answered.

Hapu and Karoya looked at Ramose doubtfully. Ramose actually didn't have any ideas for a cover story. He was tired of sneaking and hiding, tired of hiding from his enemies. He was ready to face them—the sooner the better. He just had to work out how to go about it.

They found themselves at the foot of the temple walls. The dazzling white walls loomed above them.

"What is your business in Abydos?" demanded a stern voice behind them.

The three friends turned. A man in a perfectly white kilt without a crease stood glaring at them. He had a shaved head which shone in the sunlight. His eyebrows and eyelashes had also been removed. This told Ramose that the man was a priest.

"I'm a scribe," said Ramose, not knowing what else to say.

The priest was puzzled. From the stranger's clothing, he was probably expecting Ramose to have the harsh tones and ugly accent of a foreigner. Yet Ramose spoke in perfect Egyptian with the grammar of a scholar.

"You can't be the scribe we're expecting," said the puzzled priest. "You're far too young."

The priest was waiting for an answer. Ramose didn't know what to say.

"No, he's not," Hapu said, suddenly. "The scribe had an unfortunate accident."

Ramose and Karoya looked across at Hapu in surprise.

"Yes," continued Hapu, "the scribe's right hand was crushed when a block of stone fell from a sled."

"How unfortunate," said the priest, still frowning dubiously at the strangers.

"This is the scribe's apprentice," said Hapu.

The priest looked at Ramose's nomad coat and his worn sandals.

"I am not at all sure that an apprentice can take the role of temple scribe," he said, scratching his shaved head.

Hapu thought for a moment. "He was an apprentice," he said. "But now he isn't. His training is finished."

The priest peered at Ramose again. Ramose thought that after his recent adventures he must look at least five years older than he actually was.

"He is the cleverest apprentice in memory," said Hapu, who seemed to be enjoying inventing a new history for Ramose as much as he enjoyed making up stories as they travelled. "The scribe is completely confident that Ramose is skilled enough to take his place."

The priest looked at Hapu. "And you are…"

"I," said Hapu, pulling himself to his full height of almost three cubits, "I am Hapu, temple artist and assistant to scribe Ramose."

The priest was still troubled by the strange clothing of the scribe and his party. "Where are you from? Somewhere in the south, beyond the cataracts?"

"We have come from Kharga Oasis," continued Hapu. "We were attacked by barbarians on the way. They took all our possessions, even our clothes, and abandoned us in the desert. We're lucky we survived."

"What were you doing in Kharga Oasis?" asked the priest, looking terrified at the thought of being lost in the desert. "I thought you were coming from Thebes."

"Scribe Ramose had to record some details about a new temple at the oasis," Hapu told him. "We were attacked as we were returning to the Nile."

"How terrible. What else can you expect from barbarians, though?" the priest said shaking his head.

While he was out in the desert, Ramose had vowed that when he became pharaoh he would tell Egyptians that nomads were not criminals and barbarians. He'd only been back in Egypt for a few hours and already he had broken his promise and was confirming the same old myths and lies.

"How did you get from Kharga to Abydos?" asked the wide-eyed priest, who, like most Egyptians, would rather have jumped into a pit of snakes than venture into the desert for any reason.

"We walked," said Ramose simply.

"Praise Amun for protecting you," said the horrified priest.

"We are very tired and hungry," said Hapu.

"Perhaps you could show us to our quarters and arrange for our servant to fetch us some food."

Karoya glared at Hapu.

"Yes, immediately," replied the priest.

The priest led them towards the first pylon of the temple of Osiris. The pylon, a gateway flanked on either side by huge tapering stone towers, was covered with carved images and hieroglyphs. They didn't enter the temple though. Instead of walking through the pylon, the priest led them around the eastern wall of the temple to a group of simpler, lower buildings where the temple craftsmen lived. They entered one of the houses. Inside it was cool and clean.

"We will need clothes," Hapu said.

The priest nodded.

"Scribe Ramose will require scribal tools, since his own were stolen," said Hapu.

The priest looked at Ramose to confirm this. Ramose nodded and smiled weakly. He was beginning to wonder what Hapu was getting them into.

"If your slave girl will follow me," the priest said. "I will provide her with all that you need."

Karoya followed the priest.

"Now what do we do?" asked Ramose, once the priest was out of sight.

"I don't know. I thought you had a plan."

"I do. I have to get to Thebes to see my father."

"And how did you imagine you would do that?"
Ramose hesitated. "I don't know."

"Well, it's time you thought about that," said
Hapu. "Staying in Abydos for a while will give
you some time to work out the best way to get to
Thebes."

"Or it will give me some time to get thrown into
prison for pretending to be someone who I'm not."

"You told him you were a scribe," said Hapu,
defensively. "I just...added a few details."

Servants arrived with terracotta jars of water
for bathing. Others followed with food—the sort
of food they hadn't seen for months: grapes and
watermelon; freshly baked pyramid-shaped
loaves of bread; lentils flavoured with cumin;
roast goose and a salad of lettuce, cucumber and
spring onions.

Karoya returned with clean clothes. Although
they were all hungry, they were eager to wash off
the dirt and sweat from their long journey. Once
they were clean and wearing soft linen garments,
they ate the food.

Ramose was glad to be dressed in Egyptian
clothes again. And he was pleased to be full of
good food, but Hapu was right. He didn't have a
real plan. Now that he was getting closer to
Thebes he began to wonder what exactly he was
going to do.

"I have to think of a way to get inside the

palace," Ramose said. "I have to see my father without the vizier knowing."

"You'll need a disguise," said Hapu.

"I'm too tired to think of anything now," said Ramose. "We'll devise a plan in the morning."

"I will sleep outside, like a good slave," said Karoya.

Ramose smiled at her. "I am very glad that you are both here to help me."

Hapu unrolled his reed mat on the floor. Ramose slept on a comfortable bed with a roof over his head for the first time since he had been whisked away from the palace. It felt strange.

The next morning, Ramose was woken by Karoya bringing in breakfast. Hapu yawned and stretched and surveyed the platters of food with pleasure.

"Can't we just stay here in Abydos?" he asked, helping himself to some plum cakes.

Ramose picked up a fig and walked out into the courtyard. The morning air was already hot. He didn't like Abydos. It was a dry desert town, too far away from the river. He was just about to bite into the fig when the priest who had spoken to them the day before arrived. He handed a pen box and a palette to Ramose.

"You are to work at the Temple of Osiris," the priest said. "I will take you there."

"What, now?" asked Hapu, through a mouthful of cake.

"Yes," said the priest. "The work has been delayed for far too long already. It must be completed in time for the Festival of Osiris next month. Come."

The priest turned and marched off. Ramose and Hapu had no choice but to follow him. He led them to the pylon. Guards allowed the priest to enter. They walked through the huge gateway. Through the pylon, they found themselves on a long avenue lined on either side with enormous sphinxes made of red granite.

The avenue led to the second pylon. They passed through this gateway and finally entered the temple itself. Inside it was cool and dimly lit by small windows high above their heads.

Temple workers were busy going about the daily business of the temple. Young women passed by carrying baskets of food-offerings on their heads. The sound of chanting and the smell of burning incense drifted from chambers that they passed.

The ancient temple of Osiris was being repaired. Ramose had to record the progress of the work and ensure that the architect's instructions were followed.

After half a day of writing out the texts to be carved on the walls in hieroglyphs, Ramose looked at his ink-stained hands and threw down his reed pen.

"I can't stay here," he said to Hapu, who was managing to look busy while doing nothing at all. "I have to get to Thebes. I have to see my father."

"What are you going to do, run to Thebes?" said Hapu. "If we work here for a while, we'll earn grain which we can exchange for passage on a boat."

"It will be too late by then, I know it," said Ramose. "I'll go to the river and stow away on a boat."

"I don't think that's a good idea," said Hapu.

Ramose was already on his way out of the temple, though. Hapu hurried after him. The guards at the temple gate glared at them suspiciously as they passed. Ramose headed back to the house where they were staying. Karoya was kneading dough.

"What are you doing back so early?"

"We're leaving," said Ramose.

"But—"

"We're leaving now."

Karoya didn't argue further. She put her kneading stone in her bag. She wrapped the bread dough in a cloth and put that in the bag as well.

"Leave the nomad coats," said Ramose picking up his reed bag. "We don't want to look like we're leaving. We have to pretend we're going to a job outside of the city."

Ramose strode down the street with his pen box and a piece of papyrus in his hand. "Don't look so guilty, Hapu. Pretend it's a game."

Hapu changed his expression from that of a guilty thief to that of a rich and haughty merchant. Ramose laughed at his friend. He was still smiling when they reached the edge of the city, walked out of the gate and found two temple guards waiting for them. One of the guards grabbed Ramose. The other one held Hapu and Karoya.

"What are you doing?" shouted Hapu, though he had a good idea.

The priest came out of the shadows of the city wall. One of the guards took Ramose's pen and papyrus. The other guard pulled the dough from Karoya's bag.

"You are under arrest for stealing temple property," the priest said.

"I knew we'd end up in prison," moaned Hapu.

They weren't taken to prison, though. The priest led them back to the temple and set them to work again, this time with the two guards watching them.

"You will work under guard until the work is finished," the priest said. "Then we will decide what to do with you."

Ramose had no choice. He picked up his pen and went back to work.

"We'll never get out of Abydos," he said miserably as they walked under guard back to their quarters that evening. "It'll take me a month to finish the work and then who knows what they'll do with me."

"Something will turn up," said Hapu hopefully.

When they got back to the house where they were staying, the priest was waiting for them.

"Now what's wrong?" said Hapu. "Did Ramose make a mistake with one of the hieroglyphs?"

"You are under arrest," said the priest.

"You don't have to remind me," said Ramose angrily. "I haven't forgotten that you arrested me this afternoon."

"There are new charges against you," replied the priest.

"What?" asked Ramose with a growing sense of dread.

"You are charged with impersonating a temple scribe," the priest said. "Guards, take them to the high priest."

The high priest was seated on a high-backed chair which was placed on a raised platform. He had a slender sceptre in one hand. Draped over his left shoulder was a leopard skin. The animal's head was still attached. Its dead eyes seemed to stare straight at Ramose.

The guards forced the boys to their knees. The high priest stood up and walked over to them, looking at them with distaste. "Which one is the impostor?" he asked.

One of the guards pointed to Ramose.

"He's not an impostor," said Hapu. "He's a replacement. We told you, the scribe was injured."

"Really?" said the high priest circling around the pair like a vulture. "I don't believe that a grubby wretch who wanders in from the desert is a temple scribe."

"Are you suggesting we're lying?" said Hapu, who was offended that his story wasn't believed, even though not a word of it was true.

"Yes, I am," replied the high priest. "We received a letter from the vizier last week. He is searching for three young people."

Ramose went cold. A few weeks in the desert didn't mean they were out of the vizier's clutches.

"That doesn't mean it's us," said Hapu, not sounding quite as bold.

"Unfortunately for you, the real scribe arrived this morning," said the priest. "He says he knows nothing about a replacement."

Hapu's confidence evaporated like water in the midday sun. "But, there must be a misunderstanding," he stammered.

"We'll see. Here is the scribe."

A man wearing a travel cloak entered the chamber. Ramose couldn't believe his eyes.

"Keneben!" he exclaimed.

6

HOMECOMING PRINCE

KENEBEN'S MOUTH fell open as he stared in amazement at Ramose. Then he broke into a smile. Ramose couldn't help himself. He rushed up to his tutor and threw his arms around him.

"My heart rejoices to see you," he said, unable to prevent tears blurring his vision.

Ramose owed his life to the tutor. It was

Keneben who had saved him from the queen's plot to kill him. His friend had then been banished to a foreign country.

"Are you well, Keneben?"

"Praise Amun, I live, prosper and have health."

The high priest watched this display of affection with complete surprise.

"This young man claims to be a scribe, taking your place. Is this true?"

"Not exactly, High Priest," said Keneben.

Ramose's smile faded.

"I come bearing news that the young scribe is unaware of." Keneben looked at Ramose, rustling a papyrus he was holding in his hand. "I have just received news from Thebes that will bring sorrow to us all."

Keneben paused.

"Our pharaoh is gravely ill. It is expected that he will ascend to heaven before the new moon."

"May Amun grant Pharaoh long life and happiness," said Ramose.

The high priest muttered similar words. It was what all Egyptians said whenever the pharaoh's name was mentioned, but no one meant it more sincerely than Ramose. The gods had granted his wish to see his tutor again. He hoped they would answer this prayer as well.

"Though I was about to start work here at Abydos," continued Keneben, "my services are urgently required at Thebes. Those of the young scribe will be required as well."

The high priest scowled as if he were disappointed that he couldn't punish Ramose.

"For this reason, High Priest, I ask your permission that we both return to Thebes as soon as possible."

"I will arrange for your passage to Thebes."

"Thank you, High Priest."

Keneben and Ramose bowed to the high priest and left.

"Is it true, Keneben?" asked Ramose when he and Keneben were alone. "Is my father really about to die?"

"It is true, Highness," said Keneben. "I wish it were happier circumstances that had brought us together."

Ramose took his tutor's hand in his. The last time he had spoken to Keneben was at the beginning of his adventures. He had said a sorrowful goodbye to his tutor as he left Thebes to start a life in exile as an apprentice scribe.

It seemed such a long time ago, but it was not much more than a year. He hadn't heard anything from his tutor since the secret letter he'd received at the Great Place, telling him that Keneben had been banished from the palace to the distant land of Punt. The tutor's skin was darker, as if he had spent a lot of time in harsh sun. There were lines on his face where before there had been none.

Keneben listened as Ramose told him all about his adventures since they had last met.

"I used to hate studying," said Ramose, "but there have been many times in the past months that I would have done anything to be back in the schoolroom copying texts."

"It has been difficult for you, Highness," said Keneben. "No prince should have to endure such hardship."

"What about you, Keneben?" Ramose asked.

"I worked as a scribe in Punt for many months," Keneben told him. "It was a most unhappy time."

"But now you've returned," said Ramose. "I saw you on the royal barge a few weeks ago. I knew that you were back from Punt and in favour with my sister again."

Keneben's grim mouth melted into a smile. "Yes. It was thanks to the efforts of your sister, Princess Hatshepsut, that I was able to return to the palace. She told the vizier that her studies were not progressing with the new tutor they had employed. She insisted that I teach her. I have been back at the palace now for several months."

The tutor's face flushed as he spoke of the princess. She had always had that effect on him.

They talked until late that evening. Ramose was unwilling to let Keneben out of his sight in case he disappeared again. It was a long time since he'd had news from the palace. He heard how his sister had grown tall and slender, how she had become even more beautiful, how her penmanship was the best Keneben had seen.

For Ramose, the palace had been a fading memory. There had been blank spaces in his memories, people and places that he could no longer picture. Now he could picture it all in detail. For the first time in months he felt like a prince again. It actually seemed possible that he would return to the palace and take his rightful place as the pharaoh's heir. He didn't want to lose that feeling.

Hapu and Karoya were asleep by the time Ramose went back to his quarters. He couldn't get to sleep. The air in the room was stifling. Eventually he climbed over the snoring Hapu and took his mattress out into the courtyard. He breathed in the cooler air and looked up at the stars. In a few days, he would be looking at the same stars from Thebes.

When he finally fell asleep, he dreamt about the riverbank at the edge of the palace gardens. There was one place where blue lotuses grew at the water's edge. In the dream, he was wading in the river, smelling the perfume of the lotus flowers. The sun was setting. He was thinking that this was strange, because the blue lotus flowers only opened in the morning. By evening they were usually closed tight. Then he looked again. The lotus petals turned into teeth and he realised he wasn't surrounded by lotus flowers but by crocodiles that were snapping at his legs.

The next day, Ramose, Hapu and Karoya were aboard a boat on their way to Thebes with Keneben. The boat was crowded with all sorts of people who were needed in Thebes. The death of a pharaoh was one of the most important events that could happen in Egypt. Though everyone prayed Pharaoh would live, preparations had to be made in case he didn't.

A strong breeze filled the sail. Ramose stood at the prow of the boat. He breathed in the cool Nile air. After travelling for so long on foot, it was wonderful to watch the fields and villages slip by so quickly. In a few days they would be in Thebes.

"You are still so young," said Keneben. "I had hoped Pharaoh would live long, so that you would be a grown man before you took his place."

"I am still young, as you say, and I may have only grown a little in height, but I have grown much in knowledge," Ramose said. "I have endured more than I thought possible, Keneben."

"You've had to look after yourself. Few princes know what it is like to be truly alone."

"I haven't been alone," Ramose said, glancing at Hapu and Karoya who were sitting further back in the boat. "I couldn't have done it without my friends."

"Your sister told me that you had loyal friends. But a prince should not have to suffer such hardship."

"It's made me stronger, Keneben. I believe I am ready to become the pharaoh, even if I am still young. If my father is ready to be united with the sun, I am ready to take my place on the throne of Egypt."

Ramose secretly hoped that the news that he was still alive would give his father a reason to hold on to life. He remembered the oracle's words. She had said he would see his father before he died. He didn't really believe that the old woman at the oasis could see people's futures, but her words encouraged him.

Ramose spent the time on the boat telling Keneben about his adventures. In his turn, Keneben recounted to Ramose all that had happened to him in Punt. Hapu and Karoya sat apart from them. In the evening, the boat was tied up and they sat on the banks of the river eating their evening meal. Ramose went over to his friends.

"I haven't seen much of you two," he said.

"You've been busy talking to your tutor," said Hapu.

"That doesn't mean that you can't sit with us."

"When you are the pharaoh," said Karoya, "you will not have time to sit and talk to slaves and apprentice painters."

"You'll be busy meeting with advisers, generals and foreign ambassadors," agreed Hapu.

Ramose had been concentrating so hard on how he would achieve his goal, he hadn't given much thought to what he would actually do when he became the pharaoh.

"I'll talk to whomever I please when I'm the pharaoh," he said grandly. "I'll free all slaves. I'll increase the wage of apprentice painters. I'll give every Egyptian free cakes on my birthday!"

"You'll be a popular pharaoh," laughed Karoya.

For the first time, Ramose allowed himself to believe that he really was going home. He chatted all evening, about going back to the palace, about sleeping in his own bed, about the jewellery he would have made for his sister.

"You'll have to discuss with the vizier how you want to rule Egypt," said Hapu.

Mention of the vizier spoiled Ramose's good mood. He hadn't considered how he would deal with his enemy when he became the pharaoh.

"I will appoint a new vizier," he said. "Someone I can rely on. Someone I can trust."

The three friends ate in silence. No matter what Ramose said, they all knew that things would be different between them once they arrived in Thebes.

Two days later there was a glint of white and gold in the distance and Thebes lay before them. Ramose's heart started to race. He would soon be home. The green fields on either side of the river stopped at the foot of whitewashed walls. A hundred or more gold-tipped flagpoles rose into the air with coloured pennants flapping in the breeze.

Among the temple buildings on the east bank Ramose could see the twin black granite obelisks that his father had raised in the temple of Amun. They were covered with carved hieroglyphs praising Amun, each symbol filled with gold paint. On the west bank was the palace and behind it the cliffs that hid the Great Place.

Gardens grew down to the edge of the river. It looked so beautiful that Ramose felt tears filling his eyes. The gardens contained the same crops as the fields they had passed, but they were carefully planned so that the squares of lettuces and onions made an attractive pattern. There were also flower gardens. The red of poppies, the blue of cornflowers, and the yellow and white of daisies added colour to the beautiful scene.

Ramose was relieved to see that the patch of lotus pads was still floating on the river in front of the palace garden. It was before noon and the flowers were reaching up to the sun with their blue petals spread wide. Children were wading in the shallows. There wasn't a crocodile in sight.

7

ASCENT TO THE SUN

THERE WAS a strange atmosphere in Thebes. The city was bustling with activity. It was an anxious time for Egyptians. Everyone hoped and prayed that their pharaoh would live, but if he didn't, all had to be ready for the smooth transition to a new pharaoh. Egypt without a pharaoh was unthinkable.

Crowds of people were coming and going—all

involved in preparations. Ramose wanted to walk around the streets of Thebes, but Keneben hurried them straight to the house of his mother. She worked in the small temple of Hapi, god of the Nile, on the west bank of the river.

"You must not go out of the temple grounds, Highness," Keneben said. "We cannot take any risks now that you are so close."

"But I want to see my sister."

"I have told Princess Hatshepsut that you are here."

"You've seen her? How is she? Doesn't she want to see me?"

"She is longing to see you, but she agrees that we should wait until the vizier is out of the palace."

At first, Ramose was happy to rest and walk among the temple buildings. It was a pleasure to stroll through the gardens that stretched right to the river's edge. He delighted in showing Karoya and Hapu the places by the river where he had played as a child. They could hardly believe that their friend was the spoilt, unpleasant boy who had enjoyed making servants' lives miserable. Ramose couldn't believe it either.

After three days, Ramose had walked every path in the temple grounds five times over.

"We have to work out a plan, Keneben," he said. "I will have to sneak into the palace without being seen. You will have to get a disguise for me."

"You must be patient, Highness," the tutor replied. "You must promise me you will wait until I am sure it is safe."

Ramose promised that he would be patient, but it was hard when he was so close to the palace. He was no longer used to doing nothing. He'd waited too long. With the whitewashed walls of his home visible from the temple gardens, the temptation was too great.

"I'm going for a walk in the gardens," Ramose told his friends.

Hapu was busy teaching Karoya how to play senet.

Ramose walked through the temple vegetable garden and fig tree grove. He wandered past the stables where the oxen were kept. He strolled near the muddy area where the goose herder led the geese down to the riverbank. Without think-ing about it, not consciously anyway, he had walked to the high wall that marked the end of the temple grounds. Beyond the wall was the palace. He walked in the shadow of the wall. He wasn't walking aimlessly now. There was some-thing he was looking for.

The wall stretched in a straight line for many cubits, then it turned suddenly at a right angle in front of him. In the corner, at the bottom of the wall, Ramose found what he was searching for. A hole had been cut at the bottom of the mud brick wall to allow water to drain from the court-yard within. It wasn't a big hole. It had been Ramose's secret way out of the palace when he was younger. Now it was going to be his way in. He looked around. There was no one in sight. He got down on his hands and knees and examined the hole. It wasn't big enough for him to fit through; he'd grown too much.

He searched the garden beds until he found a sharp stone. He started to hack at the mud brick around the edges of the hole. It was still a little damp from the last time water had washed through the hole. In a few minutes the hole was big enough for him to wriggle through.

Ramose scrambled to his feet on the other side. He was in a small courtyard. It was a place where female servants sat when they were spinning or sewing. Some herbs were growing in pots around the walls but otherwise it was empty. It was just as well. No one had complained about him being there when he was a child. They might have felt differently now that he was older.

He entered the palace. There was a sense of quiet urgency in the corridors. Servants and offi-cials moved swiftly but silently, each one with their own purpose. He felt self-conscious at first, imagining that people would notice him. But in his simple kilt and reed sandals he looked just like a servant. There were hundreds of servants in the palace. No one knew them all. He walked with the same silent purpose as everyone else. No one even glanced at him. Now that he was there, he didn't try to pretend to himself that he hadn't intended to get into the palace. He knew exactly what he was going to do. He'd known it all along really.

It was strange being back in the palace. The corridors were wide, the rooms huge. Everywhere was smooth and clean. The legs of stools were carved into elegant lion paws or gazelle feet. The backs of chairs were decorated with delicate patterns of inlaid jewels. Almost every wall, floor and ceiling was painted with bright pictures or patterns.

He entered a wide corridor. On either side there were rows of stone statues—enormous seated figures of the royal ancestors. His grandfather and his great grandfather were among them. They stared across at each other with blank unseeing eyes. Ramose barely came up to their knees.

Ramose was afraid that he would run into someone who knew him. He kept his head bowed and tried not to look anyone in the eye. Then he realised that there was no one he knew. Not a single servant or official looked familiar. It was like a dream. Everything was so familiar, yet it had changed somehow. He was a stranger in his own home.

He walked through the western hall. The floor was painted green, dotted with bright painted flowers. The huge papyrus-topped columns towered over him. They too were brightly painted, covered in paintings and hieroglyphs recounting the pharaoh's deeds. Here was a painting of the pharaoh throwing a spear. There was the pharaoh with his foot on the head of an enemy.

Ramose had walked through this hall every day when he had lived in the palace. He had hardly been aware of the paintings. Now he was dazzled by the brilliance of the colours. When he was a child, he had never thought about the size of the columns. Now, even though he'd grown half a cubit since he was there last, he felt dwarfed by the enormous pillars of stone.

He turned a corner, then another, and opened a door. He was in his own room. Except that it looked nothing like his room. Papyrus scrolls lay on a table. A young apprentice was busily copying cursive writing from a large stone flake onto a papyrus. He looked up and then ignored Ramose.

The room had been turned into a scribe's office. His soft bed had gone. So had the chests that held his clothes and playthings. The lion-footed chair wasn't there either. If it hadn't been for the paintings of the god Amun on one wall and his father hunting on the other, Ramose would have thought he was in the wrong room. He'd imagined he was coming home, but the palace didn't feel like home at all.

Ramose followed another corridor that led to the other side of the palace. This corridor was less familiar. There was a blanket of silence over that part of the palace. No one was hurrying. Ramose only passed one servant. At the end of the corridor there was a doorway guarded by two palace guards each holding a long, curved dagger. It was the door to his father's private quarters.

Ramose thought back. He couldn't remember the last time he'd seen his father. Many seasons had passed since he'd left the palace. Before that, in the innocent days when he didn't know his life was in danger, his father had been away on a campaign in Kush for many months. Before that?

He searched his memory for a time when he had been with his father. He had a picture in his mind of his father hunting hippopotamus by the riverbank. It was a clear picture. Then Ramose realised that all he was remembering was the painting of his father in his own room—or what used to be his room.

The last memory he had of being in his father's presence was when he had been summoned to these very rooms. His father had lectured him about throwing rotten figs at the kitchen servants.

His father had told him it was not the behaviour of a future pharaoh.

Ramose had vague memories of happy times playing with his brothers before they died. He could hear a tinkling laugh and smell a particular combination of perfume and herbs, which he knew belonged to his mother. He had no pictures of her in his memory, though. Now, soldiers with daggers guarded his father's chamber and he had to think of a way to get past them.

"Don't loiter in the corridor, boy," said a voice behind him.

Ramose bowed his head. He didn't have to look up to know who had spoken. It was a deep growling voice. He would have known Vizier Wersu's voice anywhere. The vizier had slipped into the corridor and crept up behind Ramose without him realising.

"Fetch me a goblet of wine," ordered the vizier as he swept noiselessly into the pharaoh's quarters.

Ramose bowed his head even lower as he turned and went towards the kitchens. He knew the way from his childhood. When he was small he'd liked to go there and watch the bread being made. The servants would make special cakes for him shaped like animals. As he'd gotten older, he'd stopped going there. Instead, he'd sent Heria to return dishes untouched when he'd demanded something bigger, better or entirely different.

He still remembered the way to the kitchens, though.

No one questioned him. He tried to stop his hands from shaking as he filled a jar with wine and returned to his father's quarters. He held the jar before him and the guards lowered their daggers and let him pass.

He entered the pharaoh's audience hall. It was smaller than the ceremonial western hall, but still impressive. The floor was painted blue to represent a pool covered with lotus pads and flowers. Fish and frogs swam in the water. Painted ducks paddled around the edges. It was beautiful. The columns in this room were more slender and made of wood. Their tops were carved in the shape of lotus buds. On the ceiling, a painting of a huge vulture with its wings spread wide scowled down at Ramose. Its wings must have been ten cubits across. Ramose walked through the hall and into the throne room where the pharaoh's throne sat on a raised platform. The empty throne glittered with gold and jewels. On the steps leading up to the platform were paintings of foreign captives on their knees, bound together with a rope around their necks. Each time the pharaoh walked up the steps he would tread on his enemies.

Ramose walked through the throne room into the pharaoh's sitting room. Gold goblets and bowls sat unused on a low table. There was a couch made of ebony with carved legs and arms. The rare wood was usually used only to make small items such as jewellery boxes. The wood in the couch was probably worth more than the gold and jewels that decorated it. Ramose thought back and could only remember a handful of times when he'd been in the room before. He picked up one of the goblets and filled it with wine.

Another doorway led to the pharaoh's bed-chamber. Ramose entered the room. Looking through his fringe he glanced over to the bed. Ramose could not see his father for the crowd of people standing around his bed. He thought for one dreadful moment that his father must have just died. He was wrong. It was a group of priests muttering prayers. Pharaoh's physician was there as well, mixing a foul-looking brown potion. The vizier was standing to one side.

Only one of the high windows was unshuttered, so the room was dim. With his head bowed low and his heart thudding, Ramose handed the goblet to the vizier. The vizier didn't even glance at him. Ramose backed away like a good servant, but when the vizier turned his attention back to the bed, Ramose sidestepped into the pharaoh's robing room.

It was unlikely that Pharaoh would ever be left alone, but Ramose had to hope. He sat in a corner and waited. Even that small, unlit room was lavishly painted. He sat down on a stool and rested his head against a wall painted with a grapevine pattern. The sound of the priests' chanting made him drowsy. The ceiling was covered with a spiral pattern. He was mesmerised by the swirling shapes. The chanting suddenly stopped and Ramose sat up with a start. Once again, his first thought was that the pharaoh had died. The priests and the doctor filed out. Vizier Wersu followed them. There was no wailing, no sounds of grief. Ramose was relieved to realise that it was only time for the midday meal.

One elderly priest was left to keep watch over the dying pharaoh. He was soon dozing. Ramose crept into the room so that he could see his father. Now he was so close he began to worry. Seeing his dead son appear at his bedside could easily make Pharaoh die of shock. He looked at the figure lying on the bed. What he saw was an old, old man. A man so thin and feeble it was impossible to imagine that he was the most powerful person in Egypt, that he was a god on Earth. The frail body looked nothing like the powerful, erect figure Ramose had just seen in the palace paintings, nothing like the memories he had of his father.

The priest's head dropped to his chest. Ramose crept to the bed. He thought that his father was sleeping, but when he leant closer, he saw that he was awake.

Ramose looked down at the old man's face. He opened his mouth but couldn't speak. Tears ran down his face and fell on the bed sheet. One tear fell on his father's hand. The hand rustled on the linen sheet like a dried vine leaf.

A pair of pale, watery eyes turned to him. The eyes looked at Ramose blankly.

"It's me. Ramose, your son. I didn't die. There was a...misunderstanding. I have travelled. I have learned much."

Ramose gently took the dried-up hand in his. "Father, I don't want to alarm you. I know you are ill, but I have to speak to you."

The eyes stared at him unblinking. His father had no idea who he was.

"Father, I am Ramose. I have come to take my place as your elder son...as your heir."

The dry, white lips moved, but no sound came out.

"Are you thirsty, Father?" asked Ramose.

He hurried out to the sitting room. The jar of wine he had brought from the kitchens was empty. He poured out a goblet of water instead.

"Here," he said. "There's no wine, but the waters of the Nile taste better than wine."

The old man raised his head a finger-width, but could get no further. Ramose helped him to sit up.

He held the goblet to his father's lips. A few drops of the water trickled into his mouth. His tongue ran along his lips moistening them with the river water. The old man's eyes found Ramose's again. He looked at him for a long time.

"Ramose," he whispered. The words came slowly as if each one was a great effort. "I have looked forward to meeting you and your brothers in the underworld."

"Yes, Father," said Ramose, his heart beating fast, tears running down his face. "It's me, Father. But I'm alive. I've been in hiding."

The old man smiled at his son. He raised his frail hand. Ramose felt the dry skin gently rasp his cheek. Then his eyes closed, his hand dropped to the bed. Ramose felt the body in his arms turn from a living thing to a lifeless shell as the spirit left. He laid his father down gently. His face still held the trace of a smile.

8

GHOST IN THE
SCOOLROOM

SOMEONE HURRIED into the room. Ramose
didn't move.

"Ramose," the person said. "I thought I
would find you here."

It was Keneben.

"My father is mingling with the sun," said
Ramose. "He's dead."

"May Amun protect him."

Keneben touched Ramose's shoulder. "You can't stay here, Highness. It is too dangerous."

Ramose looked up at his tutor. He wasn't sure how long he'd been sitting there in silence at the side of his dead father. It could have been a few seconds or an hour.

"I wanted to tell father about my adventures," said Ramose softly. "When I was young, he always thought I was foolish. I wanted him to be proud of me."

"Priest," said Keneben sharply. "Wake up, priest. Pharaoh has rested from life."

The priest woke with a jolt. He looked from the stern face of the tutor to the servant boy weeping silently over the lifeless form of the pharaoh.

"Don't just sit there, Priest!" said Keneben. "Get the physician."

The priest tripped on the hem of his robes as he stumbled out of the room.

"Come, Prince Ramose," said Keneben. "We must plan what to do next."

"I have to see my sister," said Ramose. "I have to tell her."

"Princess Hatshepsut is not in the palace." Keneben's voice softened when he spoke of the princess.

"Where is she?"

"She is at the women's palace."

"Why isn't she at father's side?"

"Queen Mutnofret found it too distressing to be near the pharaoh in his illness. She insisted that the princess went with her."

The women's palace was an hour's journey by boat south of Thebes. Ramose's sadness was replaced by anger at the mention of the hated queen's name.

"I have to go to Hatshepsut," he said, rushing to the door.

"Wait, Highness," said Keneben, holding out a hand to stop him. "I will send a message to her. She will return immediately."

"But the new pharaoh must be proclaimed tomorrow at dawn. I have to reveal myself."

"It is a long time till dawn. We have to keep you safe till then."

Ramose hesitated at the door.

"Wait until Princess Hatshepsut returns. With her support you will be safe."

Ramose sighed.

"You must go back to my mother's house, Highness," said Keneben. "Your friends are concerned about you."

The thought of seeing his friends again warmed Ramose's chilled heart. He turned to his father's body.

"I don't want to leave Father alone though. Will you stay with him until the priests return?"

Keneben seemed reluctant to let his young

master out of his sight, but eventually agreed to meet Ramose back at his mother's house.

Ramose walked cautiously through the corridors of the palace. He didn't want to run into the priests or the vizier. The palace was massive, bigger than many of the towns he had passed through on his travels. He chose a different route to reach the servants' quarters.

First, he went through a side door in the pharaoh's audience hall that led to a private courtyard. Then he walked down the narrow path that the gardeners used to reach the courtyard because they were not permitted to walk through the pharaoh's quarters.

He climbed over a low wall into an open area where the pharaoh's horses were kept. Beyond the stables was the wing of the palace that used to be known as the princes' palace. That was where his own room was and where his older brothers quarters had been before they died. It was also where the schoolroom was. As Ramose passed the familiar door, he couldn't resist peering in.

The schoolroom hadn't changed at all. There were no bright wall paintings there, just plain, whitewashed walls. On one wall, some hieroglyphs had been hastily drawn in charcoal. Ramose recognised Keneben's handwriting. He often used the walls to demonstrate the correct way to draw a particular hieroglyph. A papyrus was pinned to another wall. Ramose looked closer. It was the one about the benefits of being a scribe, Keneben's favourite text. There were reed mats on the floor for students to sit on. The only furniture was the graceful chair where Hatshepsut sat. He was pleased to think that his sister had kept up her studies. He was sure that she would be a valuable adviser to him when he became pharaoh.

Ramose was suddenly aware that he wasn't the only one in the room. He spun round. A young boy was standing in the doorway with an elegant ebony palette and pen box under his arm. When the boy saw Ramose's face, he dropped the palette and it shattered on the floor.

"Ramose?" said the boy in a faltering voice. "Is that you, Ramose?"

It was Tuthmosis, Ramose's half-brother, the snivelling son of Queen Mutnofret.

"Are you a ghost?" he said in a frightened voice.

"No," replied Ramose coldly. "I'm real."

The boy rushed towards Ramose who stood ready to defend himself. But the boy didn't attack him, instead he flung his arms around his neck.

"You're still alive!" Tuthmosis said. "I can't believe it."

"That's right." Ramose pulled the boy away. He was surprised to see a smile on his face. "That's the end of your scheme."

"What scheme?" The boy's brow creased.

"Well, I suppose it's your mother's scheme."

Tuthmosis looked genuinely puzzled.

"I've come to take my rightful place as the pharaoh," Ramose said.

The boy smiled again. "That's wonderful."

"Don't play act with me," said Ramose angrily.

"Where have you been these past seasons?" continued Tuthmosis. "Mother told me you'd died. Wait till she hears—"

"I know all about the plan to kill me."

"Who tried to kill you?" asked the prince, grabbing hold of Ramose's arm.

"You know very well who. Your mother."

"Don't be silly, Ramose. Why would she do that?"

"So that you could be the pharaoh."

The boy laughed. "But I don't have to be the pharaoh now. You're here."

"Don't you want to be the pharaoh?"

"No! Ever since you...died...I haven't been allowed outside the palace. I'm not permitted to play with the other palace children and I can't visit the servants' quarters any more. I have to spend more time here studying, so that I can be a great pharaoh like father. I hate it."

Ramose didn't know what to say. He thought the boy must be lying, but he didn't think he was clever enough to put on such a convincing display.

He heard footsteps in the hall. "We need to go somewhere where we can talk without being disturbed."

"I know a place," said Tuthmosis.

Ramose could scarcely believe he was allowing the young prince to lead him by the hand, but he did. Tuthmosis led him to a narrow staircase that went up to the roof. He zigzagged across the roofs until he came to the western hall, which rose up higher than the other buildings. More steps led to a ledge where a shuttered window let light into the vast hall below. There was a stool in a corner that couldn't be seen from anywhere in the palace.

"I come here when I want to get away from everyone," said the young prince.

Ramose couldn't believe it. He had used the same hiding place when he was younger.

Ramose sat down on the dusty stool and looked at the boy. He had grown taller since he'd seen him last. He had lost all his puppy fat. The mischievous glint in his eyes had been replaced with a worried, almost frightened look. His fingernails were bitten down.

"What has happened to you over the past year, Brother?" the boy asked eagerly. "Tell me everything."

Ramose told him all about the attempt to kill him, his escape to the Great Place, his journey towards Memphis to see Pharaoh, his adventures at the pyramid and in the desert. Tuthmosis sat with his mouth open, listening to everything with amazement.

"But who would want you dead?" asked the boy with tears in his eyes.

"I believe it was your mother and the vizier who planned to murder me," said Ramose.

Tears flew in all directions as Tuthmosis shook his head vigorously.

"No, that can't be. Mother wouldn't do such a terrible thing."

"I think she would do anything to make you pharaoh, and with the vizier encouraging her..."

"But I don't want to be the pharaoh."

"There is something else, Pegget," said Ramose.

Tuthmosis smiled and wiped away his tears. "You haven't called me that since I was a small child."

The word meant frog. "It isn't a very nice name, I suppose," said Ramose, feeling guilty.

"I like it," said Tuthmosis. "It's the sort of name an older brother should use for his younger brother."

Ramose felt even guiltier. He had never thought of Tuthmosis as a brother. Not like his older brothers. And yet they had the same father. He could see they both had the same large ears, long fingers and a way of turning their mouths down instead of up when they smiled—just like their father.

"What else do you have to tell me?" Tuthmosis asked. "I hope it's not as upsetting as the rest."

"It is worse, Pegget," Ramose replied. "It's Father, he has ascended to the sun. He died at midday. I was with him."

Tears flowed again from the boy's eyes. Ramose put his arm around his brother's shoulder.

"You've come just in time then," said the boy wiping his eyes on his kilt. "You can take your place as Pharaoh's elder son and heir."

"I have to wait until our sister returns to the palace. I need her support."

Tuthmosis nodded, though he looked a little timid at the mention of Hatshepsut.

"Your mother won't be so pleased to see me, though," said Ramose.

"It doesn't matter. You're here. You are the true heir. There's nothing she can do to change that."

Ramose wasn't so sure.

"I'll stay in hiding until just before dawn," said Ramose.

Tuthmosis hugged his brother. "I'll do whatever I can to help you. May the gods protect you."

Ramose turned and left. He didn't know what to think. He wanted to believe that Tuthmosis was telling the truth, that the boy didn't know about the poisoning, that he didn't mind if he wasn't the pharaoh. Ramose stumbled down the steps in confusion—and into the arms of two palace guards.

The guards each grabbed hold of one of Ramose's arms.

"Let me go," he yelled. "Do you know who I am?"

One of the guards chuckled to himself. The other took a wooden club from his belt and Ramose watched as it curved towards him and crashed into his head.

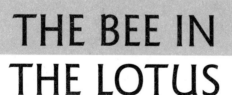

9

THE BEE IN
THE LOTUS

RAMOSE AWOKE to find himself in a dark room with his arms and legs tied up. The walls were roughly plastered with mud. Faint light seeped in through the cracks in the door. The earth floor was covered with straw that smelt of pig urine. It wasn't a room, it was a pigsty.

He wriggled his hands and feet to try and free

himself from the ropes, but all that did was make his wrists and ankles sore. He thought back to his meeting with Prince Tuthmosis. The boy had tricked him with his hugs and his tears. It must have all been a sham. Without Ramose noticing, the boy had somehow alerted the guards to come and capture him. He felt foolish that he had fallen for such a ploy.

Struggling to his knees, Ramose shuffled around his prison. He searched every finger-width of the foul place in search of something that could cut through the ropes. There was nothing. He strained against his bonds until his wrists were bleeding, furious that he'd been bound and imprisoned like a foreign captive, like a pig ready for slaughter. In anger and frustration, he threw himself against the door again and again until he fell back to the stinking floor, exhausted.

He had to think. Anger would achieve nothing. He only had a few hours until the succession ceremony that would proclaim the next pharaoh. He had to get out of his prison. He couldn't think of anything he could do. The light seeping in through the cracks faded.

The sound of a bolt sliding startled him. A servant entered holding a lamp. The light reflected in his frightened eyes. Another servant followed carrying a bowl and a cup. He put them down in the straw. Neither said a word, but outside Ramose could hear a voice—a stern female voice.

"He must stay there until after dawn." The voice sent a cold shiver down his spine. It was sweet sounding, but cruel at the same time. "If he escapes, you won't see another morning."

Ramose knew the voice. He knew it well. As the servants hurried out, Ramose could see briefly through the doorway. There was a blur of bright white in the lamplight, a flash of gold, a glint of turquoise. There was a waft of perfume. Ramose tried to cry out but his voice caught in his throat. It was Hatshepsut, his sister. She was the one who had imprisoned him.

Ramose sat in the dark and tried to make sense of it. Perhaps he was mistaken. Perhaps he'd misheard what she'd said. Perhaps it wasn't her he'd seen at all. It had just been a glimpse, a few seconds in dim light. He argued back and forth with himself for some time, but in his heart he had no doubt. His sister had betrayed him.

Through all the time that he had been away, Ramose had endured the hardship and disappointment with the thought that his sister was waiting for him, missing him, praying for his safety. It had helped to keep him going. But all that time she had kept a terrible secret. She didn't want Ramose to be the pharaoh at all. Instead it was the half-brother who they had both despised that she wanted to rule Egypt. Why? Did she hate him so much? Did she think Tuthmosis would make a better pharaoh?

Everything Ramose believed had been turned upside down. He slumped to the floor, his face in the foul straw, and wept. He cried out in pain and misery. He was alone in the world, completely alone. His loved ones had slowly been stripped away from him one by one. First, his mother, whom he could hardly remember. Then his older brothers, then Heria, his beloved nanny, and, only hours ago, his father. Now he had discovered that his only remaining family, his sister whom he had trusted completely, had turned against him.

Ramose thought of Keneben; perhaps he would come and free him. His tutor had risked everything for him before. Surely he wouldn't let him down now. But would the gentle tutor be able to stand up to the vizier and Hatshepsut? Ramose had felt lonely on his travels, but he'd always had the thought of coming home. Now he was home and he was more alone than he'd ever been. He sobbed out loud, not caring who heard him. He sobbed until every scrap of his energy was gone.

Ramose lay with his face squashed into the dirty straw for hours. His mind was blank. Every thought was painful. It was better not to think at all. His left arm was numb beneath him. His foot was prickling as if someone were sticking sewing needles into it.

He heard movement in the straw behind him, a faint rustle. He thought for a moment that there must have been another prisoner whom he hadn't noticed in the darkness. Then he saw a little creature run across the floor to the bowl of food. He could see it by the faint light from the guard's lamp that seeped in through the cracks in the door. It was a mouse. The little creature sat no more than half a cubit from Ramose's head, nibbling on a piece of bread. It was such a delicate creature, so small. Every day it had to risk its life just to feed itself. It had to creep out at night to steal food, living in constant fear of the palace cats that wanted nothing more than to crunch its fragile bones. He didn't disturb the mouse. He let it eat its fill.

Ramose suddenly remembered Karoya and Hapu. He'd been so busy feeling sorry for himself, he hadn't given a thought to them. What would Hatshepsut do with his friends? The two people in all of Egypt that he knew he could rely on, the ones who had voluntarily stayed with him through all sorts of danger and hardship. He felt ashamed that he had forgotten them.

He scrambled painfully to his knees and wriggled his fingers until the feeling came back into them. The mouse sat watching him. The mouse hadn't died, so he knew the food wasn't poisoned. He needed to eat. He had a lot to do. With difficulty he picked up the cup of water with his bound hands and drank. He picked up the remains of the bread, now dried up and mouse-nibbled. He scraped up the cold lentil stew with the bread and ate it all. It wasn't the best meal he'd ever had, but it wasn't the worst either. He sat up and felt his strength and determination return. He'd been in worse situations. He'd been lost in the desert, buried alive in a tomb, washed away by a flood. He'd survived all of that. Escaping from a pigsty shouldn't be difficult.

He picked up the empty bowl and struggled to his feet. He shuffled back and forth until he had cleared away the straw from an area of the earth floor. He raised the bowl as high above his head as he could and then with all his strength he flung it onto the cleared patch of floor. The bowl shattered. Ramose knelt down and examined the pieces. A hint of a smile crept over his face as he picked up one long shard with a sharp edge.

He sat with his back against the wall. He gripped the shard firmly between his feet and began to rub the cords that bound his hands backwards and forwards across the shard. The rope was made of twisted reeds. He cut through it fibre by fibre. It was slow work, but Ramose had no doubt that he could do it. Once his hands were free, he started to cut through the rope around his feet. The whole process must have taken two hours, but Ramose kept at it without stopping. Finally, the ropes around his ankles fell away. He walked around the cell for a few minutes until his legs lost their stiffness.

The room was built to imprison pigs, not people. The roof was low and made of two wooden beams with palm branches laid across them which were plastered over with a thin layer of mud. Ramose jumped up and grabbed at one of the palm branches. It was brittle from years of baking in the sun. It broke in half. He pulled the branch down and then another. The thin mud plaster crumbled and showered down on him. Ramose smiled to himself as he looked up at the black sky pricked with the light of the numberless stars. He jumped up again and grasped hold of one of the solid wooden beams with both hands. Then he swung up his leg. He hooked his foot around the beam at the second go and gradually managed to hoist himself up.

He inched his way along the beam. A thin sliver of moon was reclining low in the sky. It gave next to no light but there was enough light from blazing torches dotted around the palace walls for him to get his bearings. The preparations for the dawn ceremony were underway. Ramose guessed it was less than two hours before dawn. There wasn't much time until the ceremony began, but first, Ramose had something to do. He had to find out if his friends were safe.

He jumped down from the pigsty roof. But instead of heading towards the western hall, he turned the other way and retraced his steps towards the temple. He found the servants' quarters, slipped through the hole in the wall and ran through the darkened gardens towards Keneben's mother's house.

The house was in darkness. Ramose crept in. He tiptoed to the room where he and Hapu had slept. Hapu wasn't there. He went up the garden steps to the roof. Karoya wasn't there either. Their bags were gone. There was no sign that they had ever been there. He went back down the steps and into the house. Keneben's bed was empty and hadn't been slept in. Ramose had a bad feeling. If his sister had turned against him, his friends weren't safe.

By the time he had run back to the palace the area around the western hall was buzzing with activity. Ramose was puzzled. The succession was a simple ceremony only involving the new pharaoh and the head priest. It had to take place at dawn the day after the old pharaoh's death. Egypt without a pharaoh was a terrible thing. Without a pharaoh to take charge of the country, without the god-king ruling the land, Egypt would dissolve into chaos. Dreadful things would happen: disease, famine, defeat at the hands of enemies. It was vital that the new pharaoh be in place as soon as possible. The coronation itself would be a lavish ceremony with rituals, a sacrifice to the gods and a banquet lasting for days. That would wait until after the old pharaoh's funeral.

Ramose's heart was thudding, partly because he was running hard, partly because in the next hour or so he would become Pharaoh of Egypt. He would be king; he would have a place among the gods. But he didn't feel any different to any other day. There was no spark within him that might grow into a divine flame.

When he was a spoilt prince who only knew the inside of one palace or another, he had never doubted that he'd make a good pharaoh. Now, after living among ordinary Egyptians, after walking the length of Egypt, he felt decidedly un-royal, certainly not god-like. He knew more about his country and its people than he ever had before, but he'd learned how to be ordinary. What if he wasn't a good pharaoh? What if he let his people down?

He decided the best place to wait for the ceremony to start was up on the roof. He climbed up the stairs to Tuthmosis's private place. He peered through the window, cautiously. Far below in the glow of dozens of lamps, people hurried back and forth. Workmen were erecting a raised platform for the throne at one end of the hall. Chairs for officials were being arranged around the platform. Shrines and statues were being carried in. Ramose decided to wait until the perfect moment when he could walk into the hall and declare that it was his right to take his place as the next pharaoh. He pulled the stool over to where he could sit comfortably and have a good view through the window.

He woke with a start when the priests below started chanting. He had meant to stay awake, but somehow he had dozed off. The sky was a warm rosy colour. Ramose realised that the ceremony had already started. He rubbed his eyes and peered in through the window.

The hall was full of people. The government officials, leaders of the army, and two chiefs from foreign lands sat on one side. On the other side were priests, many priests. Walking down the aisle, Vizier Wersu led palace officials carrying the standards of the royal ancestors on tall poles. A high priest, with his leopard skin draped over one shoulder, followed behind. The air was thick with incense.

Behind the high priest came Prince Tuthmosis. He was being carried on a chair, not by servants,

but on the shoulders of eight government ministers. Servants on either side of him waved ostrich
feather fans.

Following the prince were Queen Mutnofret
and Princess Hatshepsut. Both were dressed in
royal splendour. They wore long dresses. The
Queen's had a pattern of snakes' heads embroidered on the hem. Hatshepsut's had a beaded
sash. Their jewellery—heavy beaded collars on
their shoulders and bracelets on their wrists and
upper arms—glittered in the lamplight.

The queen wore a wig on top of which was a
golden crown. Hatshepsut's hair had been braid-
ed into hundreds of tiny plaits. Each plait was
decorated with rings of gold placed at intervals
down its length. She wore a type of crown that
Ramose had never seen before. As well as the
raised snake's head, there was also a golden vulture's head rearing from her forehead. The wings
of the vulture, made of hundreds of tiny pieces of
jasper and lapis lazuli, draped down on either
side of her head. She carried a blue lotus flower.

His sister's face had lost all of its girlish pretti-
ness. It was still a most beautiful face, but it was
also frightening. The dark vulture's wings gave
her a threatening look. Her black-ringed eyes had
a strange, hard gloss. He didn't understand what
had happened to his sister. She had loved him, he
was sure. What had made her become so cold and

hard? Why had she turned against him? Ramose's eyes filled with tears again as he grieved for his sister's lost love. He wiped his eyes, then stood up and straightened his kilt. It was time.

All eyes were fixed on the glittering procession which had now reached the foot of the throne. The officials took their places. No one noticed Ramose enter the hall—no one except Vizier Wersu. The vizier's crocodile eyes were looking right into Ramose's. He had seen him and he knew who he was. Ramose saw the vizier turn to his men. He felt his courage fail him. It was only for a moment though. No matter what happened he knew he couldn't turn back now.

The ministers lowered the chair and Tuthmosis stepped down. He knelt before the dual shrines of Upper and Lower Egypt, barefoot and wearing nothing but a simple white kilt. Even from the back of the hall, Ramose could see the young prince shaking with fear and nervousness. The splendid decorations, the standards, the many priests, all dwarfed the small figure. He looked nothing like a pharaoh, nothing like a god. He looked exactly like a frightened little boy.

Two priests, one wearing the falcon mask of Horus, the other wearing the mask of the strange Seth creature, took a crown from each of the shrines—the white crown of Upper Egypt and the red crown of Lower Egypt. Other priests carried the royal crook and flail, symbols of kingship.

Ramose realised with a shock that this ceremony was more than a simple succession to prevent the chaos of Egypt without a pharaoh. This was also the full coronation rushed forward before the old pharaoh was even buried. This had never happened before. If his guess was right, Queen Mutnofret and the vizier were trying to prevent Ramose from having any chance of claiming the throne.

Ramose realised that Wersu was no longer on the stage. He glanced around but couldn't see him. The high priest stepped forward and spoke.

"Our Pharaoh has ascended to heaven. He is united with the sun." The priest's voice echoed around the hall. "Now the sun disc has risen from the land of light, the gods must choose a new pharaoh."

Ramose was just about to shout out and make his presence known when two things happened. First he saw two faces in the crowd that had been hidden from his view up on the roof. A chill crept over him. The faces belonged to Keneben and Hapu. Keneben was staring adoringly, not at the future pharaoh, but at the figure of Princess Hatshepsut who was sinking gracefully onto an elegant throne-like chair at the side of the platform. Her women arranged the folds of her gown.

She slowly raised the blue lotus flower to her nose to inhale its fragrance. Hapu was looking at her as well—not in admiration, but in fear. The words of the oracle came back to Ramose: the blue lotus can hide a bee in its petals. His sister had turned Keneben against him. After his years of loyalty to Ramose, he now supported Tuthmosis. Poor Hapu was powerless against her. Perhaps he too would fall under her spell. The sting of this bee was far worse than the scorpion sting.

The second thing that happened was a faint, hoarse voice behind him calling out his name. Ramose turned. A line of criminals was being led past the hall. Their hands were bound behind them. They were linked together like animals by a rope around their necks, like the figures of the enemies of Egypt painted on steps for the pharaoh to tread on.

There were two Egyptians, each with a hand or an ear cut off, indicating that they had already committed other crimes. There were three Libyans. Ramose recognised them by their beards, their long hair and the bands of leather that crossed their chests. Behind them were four people from Kush, easily recognisable by their black skin. The last one in the line was Karoya. She was staring pleadingly at Ramose. They barely had time to exchange a glance before the other prisoners yanked her along. Stumbling to her knees and struggling to regain her footing, she was dragged off around a corner.

Ramose heard his half-brother speaking in a quavering voice.

"Hear me, mighty Ra. I stand before you, ready to take my father's place."

Ramose looked back at the empty passage where Karoya had just stood, dirty and dishevelled, with her dress torn and a look of terror in her eyes. He had a decision to make—a decision that would affect the rest of his life.

More of the oracle's words came back to him. "A perfect jewel will remain buried in the earth, yet the maid at the millstone holds it out in her hand." Suddenly, he knew what the oracle had meant. Friendship was more precious than any jewel, more important even than becoming the pharaoh. He ran out of the hall after Karoya. She was a true friend. He had to help her.

Ramose had seen criminals and foreign captives taken away before. They were put in boats and taken somewhere to the south. He didn't know where. Whether they were imprisoned, enslaved or executed, he had no idea. Such things hadn't interested him before. He had to get to the palace wharf quickly. He knew every palm-width of the palace better than any servant did because he had access to all the royal apartments. He knew the palace better than any official because as a child he'd wandered through the servants' quarters and the kitchens. There was no one who knew the palace better than Ramose.

He ran through back corridors to the kitchens where he stole a sharp cutting stone. He crossed forgotten courtyards, scurried across roofs and reached the palace wharf before the guards and their prisoners. A boat was being prepared for sailing. Ramose managed to slip aboard while the boatman was attending to the sail. He hid at the stern beneath one of the rowers' benches.

It wasn't long before the guards arrived with their prisoners, swearing at them and pushing them to make them hurry. They seemed to take particular pleasure in pushing and prodding Karoya. Ramose wanted to jump out and attack the guards, but he knew that wouldn't help. He had to work out a way to get Karoya free, but not end up tied to the chain of prisoners himself.

The captives were pushed on board and the guards undid the cords binding their wrists. The prisoners were to row themselves to whatever punishment awaited them. One guard stayed on board. The other returned to the riverbank and gave the order to cast off. The boatman untied the boat and took his position at the rudder. The guard gave another order and the prisoners began to row. Karoya was sitting on the last bench. Ramose touched her foot. She jumped up with a squeal.

"Sit down, slave girl," shouted the boatman. "You'll do your share of the rowing or I'll toss you over the side."

Karoya looked at Ramose with eyes like a rabbit about to have its neck broken. He gave her what he hoped was an encouraging signal, though he didn't really have any idea what he was going to do.

Once they had drawn clear of Thebes, the guard sat down and pulled some bread and figs from a bag at his feet. Ramose leapt out. The boatman cried out in surprise and let go of the rudder. Ramose gave him a hefty push and the boatman pitched into the river.

The guard, with his mouth full of bread and a fig in each hand, moved clumsily to unsheathe his dagger. Ramose was quicker. He grasped the handle of the dagger and pulled it out. The guard made a grab for him and Ramose swung the dagger, cutting deep into the guard's fleshy arm. As the guard cried out and grabbed his arm, Ramose elbowed him in the stomach as hard as he could. The guard tumbled into the fast-flowing waters with an enormous splash.

The prisoners were all staring in astonishment, their oars hanging motionless. The boatman was trying to clamber back over the side. The guard surfaced, spluttering and swearing, and started to splash back towards the boat.

"Row!" shouted Ramose, stamping on the boatman's fingers so that he let go and fell back into the river. "Row!"

The startled prisoners rowed for all they were worth. When they were clear of the struggling guard and boatman, Ramose made them row to the shore. He cut Karoya free and handed the blade to the nearest captive. He and Karoya jumped ashore and the prisoners rowed off. Ramose hoped they found freedom.

"We have to get back to the palace," Ramose told Karoya. "The coronation is taking place."

Karoya didn't understand what he meant.

"Pharaoh has died. They're crowning my half-brother this morning—now."

Ramose turned to run back to the palace and found himself face to face with the vizier.

10

FRIENDS AND ENEMIES

VIZIER WERSU had his ceremonial sceptre in his hand. He raised it above his head ready to use it as a weapon. Ramose remembered the vision in the desert—the vizier hitting him with the Seth statue. Behind him Karoya screamed. The guard that they had pushed overboard had crawled ashore and grabbed her by the ankle. The vizier suddenly rushed forward. He moved fast, like a crocodile striking. The sceptre fell, a bronze blur. Ramose flinched, expecting the sceptre to crash down on his head, but to his surprise, it didn't. It fell on the guard, knocking him back into the river.

"Come quickly," the vizier said. "You don't have much time. The new pharaoh is about to be proclaimed."

Ramose didn't move. He stared at the crocodile-faced vizier. Why was his enemy helping him?

"Come, Highness." Ramose felt the vizier's insect fingers clutch at his arm. Ramose hesitated, unable to believe that the man he had feared all his life was now on his side. Then he remembered the oracle's words—trust the crocodile. Karoya pushed him from behind.

"Hurry, Ramose."

Ramose ran, spurred on by the vizier in front and Karoya behind. Three palace guards marched towards them at one stage, but the vizier ordered them to search the river for the missing slaves. Ramose's head was spinning. There had to be another explanation for this. It had to be a trap. It wasn't possible that the vizier was helping him.

They reached the hall. Tuthmosis was seated on the throne. He now had a deep collar made of gold and turquoise resting on his shoulders. His arms were crossed over his chest. In one hand he held the royal crook, in the other the flail. The falcon-headed priest placed the white crown on his head. The Seth-beast priest placed the red crown on top of it. Together they formed the double crown of all Egypt. Ramose opened his mouth to shout out an objection. At that moment a ray of sunlight shot down from one of the high windows. The light illuminated the dust and incense smoke in its path, turning them into beautiful golden specks and swirls. The golden ray fell on Tuthmosis's head.

"Hail Tuthmosis," said the high priest. "King of Upper Egypt, King of Lower Egypt, Chosen of Ra, Beloved of Amun, strong in truth, protector of Egypt, subduer of her enemies."

Everyone in the hall responded. "Hail Tuthmosis."

Ramose walked up towards the platform. Like everyone else, his eyes were on Tuthmosis. The boy seemed to have grown in the short time Ramose had been out of the hall. The sunlight reflected on the gold of the crook and the flail and the snakehead on the double crown. It turned Tuthmosis's skin to gold as well. He no longer looked frightened.

Ramose realised he was too late. The gods had selected their pharaoh. It was stupid of him to think that he could have influenced the will of the gods. He kept walking until he was at the foot of the platform. Priests started forward to grab him. Tuthmosis stood up.

"Leave him alone," he said. Even his voice was stronger.

The priests obeyed their pharaoh and let Ramose approach the platform. Tuthmosis held out the crook to Ramose, offering it to him. Ramose walked up the two steps.

"Hail Tuthmosis," he said so that everyone could hear him. "Pharaoh of all Egypt."

He knelt at his brother's feet. The oracle's final words echoed in his mind—bow down before the frog.

"You are Pharaoh, Pegget," Ramose said in a quieter voice so that only his brother could hear him. "It is the will of the gods. I am here to serve you."

"Are you sure, Ramose?" asked Tuthmosis. "Is this what you want?"

Ramose nodded.

"But what will become of you? What will you do?"

"Might I suggest, Highness, that Prince Ramose be proclaimed as your adviser?"

Ramose and Tuthmosis turned. It was the vizier, who had slipped back into his position on the platform. There was a murmur of surprise in the hall as people realised who Ramose was.

Both boys nodded.

"Swear him in immediately, Vizier Wersu," said Tuthmosis.

The high priest opened his mouth to object.

"High Priest," said Tuthmosis in his new commanding voice. "Say a prayer to bless my adviser."

The high priest bowed in obedience. The vizier muttered a few important sounding words. The high priest said a blessing. Tuthmosis raised Ramose to his feet.

"Hail Ramose, Fan-bearer on the Right of the Pharaoh," said the vizier.

The crowd responded. "Hail Ramose."

Not everyone joined in the response this time. Ramose could see his sister and Queen Mutnofret staring at him with tightly closed mouths.

Tuthmosis climbed back onto the chair and was carried out into the sunlight. Four geese were released symbolising that news of the new pharaoh was to be carried to the four quarters of heaven. The pharaoh himself was to be taken across the river and carried around the walls of the Temple of Amun, so that the people of Thebes could honour him. After that he would have to travel throughout the land so that all Egyptians would know that chaos and disaster had been averted. Egypt had a new pharaoh.

Ramose lay on the bed in a guestroom in the palace, trying to make sense of everything that had happened. After months of endless waiting, after weeks of wandering about Egypt at a snail's pace, his world had changed in a matter of hours. He stared up at the bulls' heads painted on the ceiling. His dream of becoming the pharaoh was over. His half-brother was now king of all Egypt. Keneben, the tutor who had risked his life for him before, now served his sister. He still hadn't spoken to Hatshepsut, and now he wasn't sure if he wanted to.

There was a knock at the door and Vizier Wersu entered. That was another thing he'd been trying to come to terms with. This man, who, since his childhood, Ramose had considered to be his worst enemy, had turned out to be a friend.

"I have been unable to arrange a meeting with your sister, Your Excellency," he said, bowing.

Ramose sat up. "Where is she?"

"She has left for the women's palace again. She won't return until your father's funeral."

"Sit down, Vizier. There are some questions I'd like to ask you."

The vizier gathered his robes over one arm and sat down on a stool.

"What is it you want to know, Highness?"

"How exactly did you discover that I was still alive?"

The vizier smiled his crocodile smile. "I have spies all over Egypt. A little gold can be very persuasive. I heard that Keneben had hidden someone in a temple and then I learned that he was secretly arranging a position for an apprentice scribe in the Great Place."

"Why didn't you come and get me back then?"

"I believed Keneben's plan was a sound one. You were far safer there than in the palace. I had tried to keep an eye on you, but I did not know that Queen Mutnofret would stoop to murder. If Keneben and your nanny had not taken the precautions they did, you would have been poisoned."

"What about when I left the Great Place?"

"I lost track of you, I am afraid. I had people searching the country, but they couldn't find you. It wasn't until I heard news of tomb robbers in Lahun that my spies tracked you down. And then you slipped through their fingers again. Your skills at staying hidden are very impressive."

Ramose laughed. "There was no skill involved. I was just blundering around the country getting into trouble at every turn."

"Praise Amun, you are safe now."

Ramose looked at the vizier. "Why did you go to so much trouble to help me?"

"I serve the royal family," said the vizier. "You were the future pharaoh. It was my job to tend to your welfare."

"Did you suspect Queen Mutnofret?"

"No, Highness. I underestimated her. I wasn't concerned for your life, just your happiness. When your mother died and then your brothers, I could see that these losses affected you more than your sister. I did what I could to make them easier to bear."

"I had no idea."

"I convinced Pharaoh to delay your military training. I stopped him from taking Keneben to Punt with him. I saw to it that Heria, your nanny, stayed in the palace long after her duties were finished."

"It's hard for me to believe you have been looking out for me all this time. I thought you were my enemy."

"It was necessary to be stern. I knew you had a difficult path ahead of you." The vizier shook his head. "I didn't know just how difficult." Wersu stood up with a sigh. He looked old and tired.

"I'm sorry I didn't recognise your concern, Vizier. I was a selfish boy then."

"In the end I failed you. You were exposed to great danger. You did not take your rightful place on the throne."

"It is the will of the gods, Vizier."

"Aren't you disappointed, Ramose?" asked Karoya, as she walked down to the palace wharf with Ramose two days later.

"No," replied Ramose. "This is what was meant to be."

"But all the time I've known you, you've been working towards taking your place as the pharaoh. It's what you lived for." She stopped and looked at Ramose. "If you hadn't rescued me, you would be the pharaoh now."

Ramose shook his head. "The gods decide who will be the pharaoh, not lesser queens, not even royal princes."

"And you're not unhappy?"

"No," said Ramose, smiling at Karoya. She was wearing a beautiful gown and shawl made of blue cloth. It wasn't in the style of Egyptian clothing. It had been especially made for her in the style of the people of Kush.

"The only thing I regret is that my sister has become a stranger to me."

"I don't understand what happened to her. When I met her, back at the tomb makers' village, she seemed kind. And she seemed to love you."

"She became greedy for power."

"But she can never be the pharaoh."

"No, but she sees Tuthmosis as being a weak boy she can control."

Karoya shook her head. "I don't understand these things."

"Neither do I. That's why I'm leaving Thebes. I don't want to spend my life among such people."

"The oracle was wrong." said Karoya. "She told us that you would be the pharaoh."

"No. She said I would achieve my goal. My goal was to see my father before he died. I achieved that. I also wanted happiness. I would never have been happy as the pharaoh, constantly at war with my sister, afraid for my life."

"But you suffered so much."

"And I learnt a lot, Karoya—about Egypt and about myself. I've realised that I'm an odd sort of Egyptian. I have a liking for travel and a desire to get to know barbarians. I would never have found that out about myself if I had stayed in the palace."

"But being a fan-bearer sounds very dull," said Karoya.

Ramose laughed. "I don't actually have to sit at Pharaoh's side waving a fan, Karoya. Fan-bearer on the Right of the Pharaoh is a title. It's one of the highest positions in Egypt, next to the vizier. And Tuthmosis is happy to let me wander around Egypt and report on the situation at its borders. So he's given me another title—Superintendent of Foreign Lands."

"I'm glad you're coming with me," said Karoya.

"My first duty will be to deliver you back safely to your people."

Vizier Wersu was waiting for them at the wharf. He smiled as they approached. Ramose still thought he looked like a crocodile, but he had learned to like the vizier.

"I have carried out your wishes," the vizier told him. "Keneben will not be banished, but he is no longer the royal tutor. He will be posted in a lesser temple."

"And Queen Mutnofret?"

"She will be confined in a remote palace," the vizier replied. "It is more than she deserves."

Ramose nodded. He hadn't been able to bring himself to demand the death sentence she deserved. She was after all Tuthmosis's mother.

"There is someone who wishes to speak to you, Your Excellency," the vizier said.

A small figure with his head hung low came from behind the vizier. It was Hapu. The boy fell to his knees.

"I'm sorry, Your Excellency," he said, with tears streaming down his face. "I let you down. I could not do anything to stop the coronation."

"Get up, Hapu," said Ramose. "And for Amun's sake call me Ramose. There was nothing you could have done."

"I could have tried at least. I was afraid of Princess Hatshepsut," said Hapu, miserably.

"You were wise to fear her, Hapu. She is dangerous."

"Why don't you come to Kush with Ramose and me?" asked Karoya.

Hapu shook his head. "I don't want any more adventures. I just wish I could go back to the Great Place and be an apprentice painter again."

"I think that can be arranged." Ramose glanced at the vizier. The vizier nodded. "It will be good to have you working on my father's tomb. You can make sure the tomb makers do the job properly."

"Thank you, Ramose."

Ramose hugged his friend and then stepped aboard the boat. Karoya followed. The vizier, who was going with them as far as the first cataract, helped her aboard.

The boat pulled away from the wharf. Ramose waved goodbye to Hapu. Earlier, he had taken leave of his brother who had hugged him and told him he would miss him. He hadn't spoken to Hatshepsut. He had glimpsed her in a corridor, but she had turned away from him.

"Was my sister involved in the plot to poison me?" Ramose asked the vizier.

"No, Your Excellency, but in the months that you were absent, she developed a greed for power. She thought that she would make a better pharaoh than you or your brother. She planned to rule from behind the scenes. Not even Queen Mutnofret realised."

Ramose sighed. His sister was lost to him, but he had a brother now. He glanced at the vizier. And he had friends in very high places.

Karoya sat down next to him. Her face showed a mixture of joy because she was going home, and terror because she had to spend weeks on a boat with the Nile in flood. The boat plunged through the surging waters. Karoya held on to Ramose's arm.

The wind filled the sail and the prow of the boat cut through the waters of the Nile. Ramose breathed in the familiar air—moist, and laden with the smell of vegetation. He turned his face to the south. He was on his way to the very edge of Egypt and beyond. And he was eagerly looking forward to it.

A WORD FROM THE AUTHOR

PEOPLE who study ancient Egyptian history are called Egyptologists. They have written books about every aspect of life in ancient Egypt. Reading these books, I was able to find out what people in ancient Egypt wore, what they ate, how they travelled. Egyptologists learned a lot of this information from the writings that they found in ruins of temples, palaces and inside the pyramids. Some of the writing was carved into stone, some written in ink on papyrus or stone chips. Fortunately the ancient Egyptians liked to write everything down, so that a lot of writings have survived.

When people first started studying ancient Egyptians, they couldn't understand their writing. A single stone inscription was responsible for unlocking the mysteries of hieroglyphics. In 1799, a stone was discovered in a village called Rosetta. On it was a decree from the year 196 B.C. The decree was written in three ways: in hieroglyphics, in demotic (another form of Egyptian writing) and in Greek. Egyptologists were able to compare the Greek writing, which they could read, to the Egyptian writing.

It wasn't easy though. More than twenty years passed before someone managed to translate the hieroglyphs. A French man called Jean-François Champollion realised that the names of pharaohs were always written inside an oval shape called a cartouche. He found that this was true on all the temples and pyramid writings as well. Using this he was able to break the code of hieroglyphics.

After that, the writing on all the tombs, temples, papyri and stone chips that had been found could be translated. People began to understand the world of ancient Egypt a lot more. If the Rosetta stone hadn't been found, we would know very little about the way ancient Egyptians lived and it would have been a lot harder for me to picture Ramose's daily life.

RAMOSE

THE WRATH OF RA

NAHARIN

SYRIA

Kadesh

Islands in the Midst of the Sea

GREAT GREEN SEA

Land of the Hyksos

Memphis

LIBYA

River Nile

EGYPT

Thebes

Pathyris

1st Cataract   Aswan

RED SEA

Buhen

N

Semna   2nd Cataract

Rebel Fort

Sai

3rd Cataract   KUSH

Tombos

4th Cataract

5th Cataract

0   500 km

100   200   300   400

Punt

HOME

THE SUN was hanging just above the horizon like a red-hot medallion. Golden light reflected on the palace walls turning them from white to pale orange. The gold tips on the flagpoles looked like they were on fire. From the prow of a reed boat, Ramose watched as the sun disappeared behind the desert hills to the west. The sun god, Ra, was starting his dangerous night journey into the underworld. The Nile was like a river of molten gold flowing around the small craft.

Ramose had seen many sunsets on his travels, but this was the most beautiful. For the first time in two years, Ramose was watching the sun set, not in a foreign place, but behind his home. He breathed in deeply. He could smell fermenting grapes, frankincense and oxen dung—the unmistakable smell of Thebes. The oarsmen guided the boat to shore. Ramose leapt ashore before the boat was tied to the wharf. He was home.

When he'd left Thebes six seasons earlier, Ramose had been happy to get away from the palace with its stiff ceremony and unpleasant politics. He had been hungry to see the world.

In the time that he'd been away, he had learned a great deal. Under his arm was a papyrus scroll on which he had written all the amazing things he had seen. On one side of the scroll, he had a list of foreign customs and a record of inventions that he thought might be useful to Egypt. In his bag, he had a collection of seeds from plants that produced all sorts of strange fruits and grains.

He was eager to tell the vizier all he had learned in foreign lands and he was confident this knowledge would benefit Egypt.

Ramose's heart was thumping in his chest as he hurried towards the palace. He remembered the last time he'd come home after a long absence. He'd had to sneak in like a thief. His own chamber had been turned into a scribe's office. He'd felt like a stranger in his own home.

He walked up to the palace gate. The timing was perfect. He would be just in time for the evening meal. His mouth watered as he imagined the trays piled with meat and vegetables straight from the palace garden. He could almost taste bread fresh from the oven and sweet honey cakes.

Two guards were standing at the outer gate. They each had long curved daggers in their belts.

"Halt and state your business," said one of the guards.

"I am Prince Ramose," Ramose replied, not without a trace of pride. "I have returned from travels abroad."

He had hardly ever used his title while he'd been away. He'd preferred to travel as an ordinary scribe. After two years of simple living, he was quite looking forward to being treated like a prince again. The guards didn't move.

Ramose held up the medallion that was hanging around his neck. "Look, this was given to me by my brother, the pharaoh," he explained. "Pharaoh is expecting me."

When he was younger, a spoilt prince who had hardly been outside the palace, this sort of incompetence would have infuriated him.

The guards peered at the medallion.

Two cobras arched on either side of it. Between them was the eye of Horus. Above were the hieroglyphs for the official title his brother had bestowed on him. The medallion was made of hundreds of tiny pieces of semi-precious stones—carnelian, turquoise, lapis lazuli—all set in gold. It was a beautiful thing, or at least it had been. Many of the jewels were chipped or had fallen out.

Ramose turned it over to show the guards the inscription. They looked suspiciously at him.

"Can't you read?" asked Ramose, his stomach grumbling at the delay. His patience was fading. He jabbed his finger at the inscription. "It says, Ramose, Fan Bearer at the Right of Pharaoh, blood of his blood, beloved of Amun."

In fact, the back of the medallion was so scratched and worn that the hieroglyphs were difficult to read in the fading light.

"I've got a papyrus too," Ramose said, reaching into the worn leather bag on his shoulder.

The guards both drew their daggers and grabbed Ramose.

"It's only a piece of papyrus. It says that I'm the Superintendent of Foreign Lands. That's where I've been for two years, in foreign lands."

Ramose tried to shake off the tight grip of the guards. "Take me to the vizier."

"No strangers to be let in," said one of the guards. "That's our orders. The palace is under tight security, because of the rebellion to the south."

"I'm not a stranger," Ramose said. "I'm Pharaoh's brother."

The guards marched Ramose from the gate, ignoring his protests.

"Get out of here." They pushed Ramose away. He stumbled on a rock and fell in the dust.

"You'll be sorry for this," shouted Ramose. "Pharaoh will punish you."

The guards went back to their post, laughing. "Imagine coming to the palace gate looking like that and saying you're Pharaoh's brother."

Ramose picked himself up. He wouldn't waste his time arguing with servants. He would get in some other way.

He walked around the palace walls, now a deep red as they reflected the last rays of sunlight. He searched the base of the wall, looking for the hole that he'd used to escape through when he was a child. He couldn't find it. Eventually he found a patch of fresh mud brick. Someone had filled in the hole.

Ramose was getting very annoyed. He hadn't expected people to be out in the street cheering, but he had thought his brother at least would be eagerly awaiting his return.

There was a small gate in the palace wall at the point where it was closest to the river. It was used by the female servants who washed clothes at the river's edge. Ramose tried the gate. It was barred on the inside. He sighed and sat down on a rock at the edge of a field of vegetables. He was running out of ideas.

Soon, Ramose's anger had turned to anxiety. What if his half-brother, the pharaoh, was trying to keep him out of the palace? There had been a time when the palace had been a dangerous place for Ramose. He had been the pharaoh's heir. It was Ramose who should have become the next pharaoh, not Tuthmosis. But Tuthmosis's mother, a lesser queen, had wanted her own son to be pharaoh. She had tried to poison Ramose. Ramose's tutor and nanny had saved him by feigning his death and sending him to live in secret in the Great Place. He had worked as a common scribe at his father's tomb for almost a year. It was there that he had stopped being a spoilt prince and learned the value of humility and friendship.

When his father had died, Ramose returned to take his place as pharaoh. But the gods had chosen a different path for him and Tuthmosis had taken his place on the throne of Egypt with Ramose's blessing. Surely there was no reason for his half-brother to turn against him now?

The gate suddenly opened a crack and a young servant girl slipped out. She didn't notice the dark figure sitting in the purple twilight. She walked quickly to the vegetable patch and knelt down to pick some lettuce. Ramose jumped up and darted in through the gate. He ran in through the courtyard and straight into the kitchens. The cooks were resting as the serving girls prepared the last trays of food to be taken to the western hall. Everyone turned as Ramose rushed into the room.

"Intruder!" shouted one of the cooks. "Call the guards!"

Ramose ran through the kitchens, out into the corridor—straight into the arms of a guard. Other guards grabbed him and he was hauled down the corridor towards the western hall.

They dragged him into the hall. Flickering flames from many torches reflected in the bright coloured paintings on the huge granite columns. The hall was full of people. Servants were serving food to a dozen or more palace officials. Dancers and musicians performed at one end of the hall, though no one was taking any notice of them. On a raised platform in the centre of the hall, a young boy sat on a throne that seemed too big for him. Despite the six anxious servants who were all on their knees offering him meat, bread, fruit and wine, the boy looked lost and lonely.

The buzz of conversation suddenly died. Everyone in the hall turned as the guards forced Ramose to his knees in front of the platform. The musicians stopped playing their lutes. The dancers stopped shaking their tambourines and rattles. A servant dropped a tray. Apricots and plums rolled across the floor.

"What's this fuss?" asked the boy crossly.

"We found an intruder in the palace, Highness," said the guards.

"I'm not an intruder. It's me, Pegget," said Ramose, calling his brother by the nickname he'd used when Tuthmosis was a toddler. Pegget meant frog.

"How dare you address Pharaoh in such an insolent way?" said one of the ministers.

The young boy on the platform stood up and looked closer at Ramose.

"Who is this?"

"Your brother," said Ramose.

"Ramose?" said the young pharaoh. "Is that you?"

"Yes," replied Ramose. "You've grown, Pegget, but I don't think I've changed that much."

Tuthmosis rushed down the steps from the platform and threw himself at his brother.

"I didn't recognise you," he said, squeezing Ramose so hard he could hardly breathe. "You look like a barbarian."

A torch flared and Ramose caught a glimpse of his reflection in a polished bronze shield hanging on the wall. He hadn't realised how strange he looked. He'd grown of course, but his face was thinner. His skin was dark. His hair had grown long, below his shoulders and he had it tied back in a plait. He wasn't wearing a white linen kilt like the other males in the hall. Instead he wore the long, dark robes that men wore in the land of Naharin.

"We weren't expecting you for another month," said Tuthmosis.

"But I wrote to tell you I'd be arriving earlier."

"I have heard nothing from you for weeks." Tuthmosis dragged Ramose up onto the platform. "Bring a chair for my brother," he demanded. "Are you hungry?"

A servant brought an elegant chair for Ramose. He sank onto it with relief.

"I'm starving," said Ramose, taking a handful of bread and meat from a tray. "Is there any gazelle milk? I haven't had any for nearly half a year."

The young pharaoh turned to a servant. He didn't even have to speak. She was already bowing and backing away.

"You must tell me everything about your journey."

"I'm eager to tell you, Pegget," said Ramose through a mouthful of bread. "Just as soon as I've eaten." He stuffed meat and salad into his mouth. Tuthmosis smiled at his half-brother.

Ramose looked around the room as he ate. He looked from face to face.

"If you're looking for Hatshepsut, she usually eats in her rooms."

Ramose had been looking for his sister. He didn't know whether he was sad or glad that she wasn't there to greet him. He searched the faces of the people again.

"I haven't seen Vizier Wersu either. Where is he?"

"He's been in Kush. He should return any day. There's been a rebellion."

Ramose turned to his brother.

"Is it serious?"

"Oh yes," replied Tuthmosis, his eyes lighting up. "I had to send two battalions of soldiers. There were battles."

"When I was in Kush, there was no unrest."

"The rebels almost took the fortress town of Sai," continued Tuthmosis.

"I haven't heard this," said Ramose. "I've been travelling far to the north of Egypt."

"Hatshepsut said if we didn't nip the bud of rebellion, they'd be attacking the palace before we knew it," replied the boy.

Ramose was surprised. Since when had his sister been a military adviser?

The hall fell silent again. Ramose looked up. A beautiful woman had entered, accompanied by six other women. Ramose glanced at Tuthmosis. The boy's smile disappeared.

The woman wore a flowing gown and exquisite jewellery on her arms and around her neck. On her head was a simple gold crown. Her hair hung like a black curtain on either side of her face. Her face was beautiful but without expression. Ramose shivered as her green-lidded eyes stared at him coldly.

She sat down on a throne-like chair, the same size as the pharaoh's. It had a high back and arms carved in the shape of crouching jackals. She looked away from Ramose and glanced over a platter of meat and vegetables. Her expression didn't change. She assessed the meat with the same cold, uninterested stare and waved it away.

Ramose was determined not to be dismissed like a plate of sliced meat. He stood up and walked over to her.

"Greetings, sister," he said. He didn't bow or kneel before her as everyone else did. "I'm glad you have chosen this evening to join our brother and eat in the hall."

He stood looking down at her, knowing that he had her at a disadvantage, but that she wouldn't stand to meet him. Hatshepsut continued to stare at Ramose with a look of distaste.

"You look like a vagabond, Ramose," said the princess as she accepted a bunch of grapes from one of her women.

"You are beautiful as always, Hatshepsut," Ramose replied, though he managed to make it sound like it was less than a compliment.

"You could have at least bathed before you joined us to eat," she said, raising one perfectly curved eyebrow as she looked at Ramose's dirty feet with disgust.

"I apologise if my appearance offends you. I was anxious to see our brother and find out if he was well."

"He is well, as you see."

Hatshepsut turned her attention to a platter of figs and dates.

"I hear that you have become one of Pharaoh's military advisers," said Ramose.

"I take an interest in Egypt's affairs, that is all. Pharaoh sometimes honours me by listening to my advice."

Tuthmosis was wriggling on his throne.

"Let's talk about the affairs of state some other time," he said, glancing timidly at Hatshepsut. "Ramose hasn't finished his dinner yet."

"I look forward to speaking with you further," said Ramose.

As he turned away from his sister, he felt a jumbled mixture of anger and sadness. She had

once been his dear sister and closest friend, someone who he trusted without question. She had
been one of his few allies at the palace in his time
of exile. Then she too had turned against him,
helping the queen in her plot to keep him from
the throne.

Hatshepsut hadn't wanted him dead. At least,
he didn't think so. But now he distrusted every
look, each word. Everything about her seemed
threatening. He had to admit that she was right
about one thing though.

"I'm going to bathe," said Ramose. "Our sister
finds my smell offensive."

He smiled at Tuthmosis. "With your majesty's
permission, I will retire."

"But you haven't told me about all your
adventures," said Tuthmosis, looking more like a
sulky child than a pharaoh.

Ramose smiled at his brother. "Tomorrow I will
be at your service from dawn till midnight."

Tuthmosis waved two servants towards them.
"Attend to my brother," he ordered.

"That won't be necessary," Ramose said. He
bowed to his brother and left the hall.

It wasn't the homecoming he'd been expecting.
He belatedly realised how strange he must have
looked to the guards and other inhabitants of the
palace. Most of them had never been outside
Thebes, let alone visited foreign lands.

He walked down the corridor, turned to the left and then to the right. He stood outside a room. He opened the door. The room was lit by two oil lamps. He walked over to the bed which was covered in smooth linen sheets. He sat down. The mattress was soft. Next to the bed was a beautiful gold-painted chair carved with elegant patterns, with legs that ended in lions' feet. On a low table there was a statue of Ra with a hawk's head. There was also a large chest made of red cedar wood. Each side had a carved ivory panel bordered by strips of ebony and turquoise. The panels showed scenes of a prince riding in a chariot, hunting lions, making an offering to the gods.

Ramose had seen many wonderful things in his travels, but no one matched the Egyptians in artistry. He opened the chest. Inside were neatly folded kilts and tunics, pure white and sweet-smelling.

A doorway led to his bathing room, where he could see large clay pots of water and containers of cleansing oils at the edge of the sunken bath. He looked at the paintings on the walls: one was of his father hunting hippopotamuses, the other of Amun, king of the gods. Ramose smiled to himself. This was his own room. He was home at last.

2

VISITORS

RAMOSE woke from a deep sleep late the following morning. He got up reluctantly from the comfortable bed and walked out into the courtyard. There was a small square pond containing fish and lotuses. In the garden beds that surrounded the courtyard, poppies were just opening. A date palm, heavy with fruit, towered overhead.

Servants entered his chamber noiselessly and laid out fresh clothes and new sandals for him. One had a comb ready to tend to his hair. Others brought platters of food. He wondered how they'd known he was up. Did they listen with their ears to the door?

"I'll dress myself, thank you," said Ramose, shooing the servants away.

The servants looked confused by the idea of a royal prince dressing and feeding himself, but they started to back out of the room.

"Don't take the food though," he said, taking the platters from them. "And bring me a sharp blade and a mirror."

Ramose couldn't imagine how he'd ever lived with servants fussing around him all day. He welcomed the lavish breakfast though. He hungrily ate plum cakes and figs and drank pomegranate juice. After he had eaten his fill, he propped up the mirror on the cedar chest and cut off his long hair with the blade.

When he arrived in his brother's rooms, Pharaoh had just returned from his early morning duties at the temple. Ramose had been hoping to speak with his brother alone, but the rooms were crowded with servants and officials planning his day.

"You look like an Egyptian again," said Tuthmosis, admiring his brother's haircut.

"I'd like to meet with the ministers to tell them what I've learned in foreign lands." Ramose smoothed his hair. "I don't want to frighten them."

"I want to hear all about your travels," said Tuthmosis. He turned to an official. "I'm going to spend the morning with my brother," he said.

"Unfortunately, Highness, you have no free time this morning," said the official, consulting a papyrus scroll. "You are receiving a general recently arrived from Libya in half an hour. You have a meeting with the governor of the Abydos district after that. Then you have your lessons. You are to take your midday meal with the high priest and then you will go to the Temple of Ptah to perform his feast-day ritual."

Tuthmosis sighed. "I never have any spare time," he said sadly. "I'll see you at the evening meal, Ramose," he added as the official hurried him out of the door.

Ramose tried all day to make an appointment with the ministers, but at sunset he still hadn't managed to pin them down. He suspected they were trying to avoid him. When everyone gathered for the evening meal though, they were not able to escape. Ramose sat next to a group of ministers and unrolled his papyrus. It was ripped and ragged, stained and worn. He asked a servant to remove some of the plates of food on a small table and laid out the papyrus, holding it down at the corners with bowls and goblets. The ministers were paying more attention to the disappearing food than to the papyrus.

At that moment Tuthmosis entered with his servants and officials. He looked weary, but he smiled when he saw Ramose.

"I will eat with my brother," he said.

Servants hastily dragged his throne down from the platform for him to sit on and held food up for him to eat.

"So, Ramose, at last I will get to hear about your travels."

"I was just about to show the ministers many things that I think will be useful to Egypt. Take for instance—"

A rustle of linen and a whiff of perfume made everyone's heads turn. Hatshepsut had entered the hall with her ever-present women. Instead of taking her usual place at the edge of the hall at a distance from everyone else, she sat where she could hear what Ramose was saying.

Ramose looked at his sister and began again.

"This is a list of devices that people in other lands use," he said pointing to his lines of small and untidy writing.

The ministers peered at the writing with puzzled looks.

"I see your handwriting hasn't improved," commented Hatshepsut.

"I wrote whenever I got the chance. Sometimes it was on a barge, sometimes on a sled pulled by a camel. It is what I have written that is important, not the neatness of the writing."

Tuthmosis was looking worried. He didn't want his brother and sister to have an unpleasant argument.

"No one need read it. You tell us all about these things, Ramose."

The ministers shifted restlessly on their stools.

"Egypt has much to teach the barbarian sand-dwellers," said one, "but they have nothing to teach us." The other ministers nodded.

Ramose tried again.

"Our fathers' fathers learned how to use horses and build war chariots from their conquerors. Isn't that right, sister?" he said directly to Hatshepsut. "They learned new skills and practised them until they were better than their masters. Then they used them to defeat their conquerors."

The ministers seemed unmoved.

"We can build chariots that are not meant for war. They have four wheels and can be pulled by oxen." Ramose enthusiastically pointed to a diagram on his papyrus. "We could use them to carry food to our settlements in the desert. One ox can pull much more weight than it can carry on its back."

"We have plenty of oxen," said Hatshepsut, "and if there aren't enough oxen, we can use men to carry things."

Ramose glared at his sister. He'd been waiting for this opportunity all day and he was determined that she wouldn't spoil it. He emptied the contents of a small bag onto the table. A handful of shrivelled-up seeds cascaded out.

"These are the seeds of many plants that we could grow in Egypt," said Ramose.

He picked one out.

"This is the seed of a fruit the colour of the sky at sunset, the colour of carnelian. Its skin is thick, but you can easily peel it off with your fingers. Inside are segments, each one filled with sweet-tasting juice."

The ministers looked blankly back at him. Ramose picked up another seed.

"This one comes from a type of tree that grows in the Islands in the Midst of the Sea. Its fruit is small, black and too bitter to eat, but if they're salted, they make a tasty morsel to eat with lettuce and cucumber."

"I'm not interested in what foreigners eat," said Hatshepsut. "Egypt provides us with plenty of food. The gods will be offended if we are not content with what they have provided."

The ministers muttered and nodded in agreement. The corners of Hatshepsut's mouth turned up slightly.

"Next you'll be telling us how much you admire the barbarians in Kush, whose men dance like women, so I've heard."

The ministers all laughed at the thought of this bizarre behaviour.

"Our father knew the only way to deal with foreigners," Hatshepsut continued. "It was at the point of a sword."

Ramose didn't want to say anything against his dead father. "Father did many great things for Egypt," he replied.

"We bring our enemies to their knees and make them bow down before Pharaoh," continued his sister. "That is how Egypt became great and powerful."

She turned to Ramose.

"If you were truly interested in the welfare of Egypt," said Hatshepsut, looking at him as if he were an unpleasant insect, "you'd be in Memphis training for military service."

"I don't want to be a soldier."

"You should be training to be a great general like our father," said Hatshepsut. "Instead, you are talking about gardening and concerning yourself with the loads of oxen. You're more like a servant than a prince."

Everyone was looking at him. Ramose felt like a scolded child. Hatshepsut rose and swept out, leaving the hall so quiet you could have heard a feather fall.

The silence was broken by the entrance of a palace official. He bowed to the pharaoh.

"The vizier has just arrived, Highness," he said. "He wishes to report on the situation in Kush."

A tall, thin man walked wearily into the hall.

"Highness," he said bowing to the young pharaoh. "Life, health, prosperity."

The last time Ramose had seen the vizier was almost a year before, when they'd met by chance in the land of Punt. Ramose thought he now looked old and tired.

"Vizier Wersu, my heart rejoices to see you," he said, embracing the old man's bony frame.

"Prince Ramose, this is a pleasant surprise," said the vizier. "You look well and healthy."

Ramose hadn't always thought of the vizier as his friend. In fact, for a long time he'd been convinced that Wersu had been involved in the plot to kill him. He'd been mistaken though. The vizier had always been watching out for him—Ramose just hadn't realised it.

"I haven't arrived alone," said the vizier, smiling his crocodile smile.

Ramose realised that someone else had entered the hall. There was a small dark figure standing in the shadows and veiled by a head-cloth. He moved closer, peering at the half-hidden figure. Bright eyes looked up at him. A dark-skinned face was suddenly split by a huge white smile.

"Karoya!" said Ramose.

Karoya came up and flung her arms around Ramose's neck.

"It's so good to see you," said Ramose. His annoyance over Hatshepsut evaporated and was replaced by delight. He hadn't realised how much he'd missed his friend.

"You remember Karoya, Pegget," Ramose said, drawing Karoya out of the shadows and in front of his brother.

Karoya bowed to the pharaoh.

"Of course I remember her," Tuthmosis replied. "What brings you to Thebes, Karoya?"

Ramose had been about to ask the same question. The last time he had seen Karoya, she was living in her homeland of Kush.

Karoya's smile disappeared like a flame dipped in water. "Nothing good, Highness," she said.

"The rebellion in Kush has made it unsafe for Karoya to stay in Sai," said the vizier.

"Is the situation that bad?" asked Ramose.

The vizier nodded grimly. "There were only a few rebels to begin with, but their numbers have grown. They have had small victories over Egyptians and these have made them bold."

Karoya looked at Ramose. He could only imagine how difficult this was for her. Although she had been captured by Egyptians and made a slave, she had become Ramose's good friend during his time in exile. Pharaoh had appointed her as a representative of her people as a reward, giving her the title of Pharaoh's Chief Envoy in Kush. She had been working in the town of Sai for the last two years, representing her people's case if there was disagreement between the Egyptians and the Kushites.

"I have come up with a strategy," said the vizier, "which I hope will bring peace to the land of Kush."

Ramose looked at the vizier. "Without further bloodshed?"

The vizier nodded. "Our soldiers managed to capture the son of one of the rebel leaders who is a Kushite chief."

"You've brought a prisoner?" asked the young pharaoh excitedly.

"He isn't a prisoner," said the vizier with a grim smile. "He is our guest."

"Where is he? I want to meet him."

"In good time, Highness."

It wasn't until the next day that Ramose got a chance to talk to Karoya alone. They walked by the river and talked about everything that had happened in their lives since they'd last met. Within half an hour, it was as if they'd never been apart.

"It's good to have your company again, Karoya," said Ramose. "I've enjoyed travelling, but I missed my friends."

"Have you seen Hapu?"

"Not yet, I only arrived yesterday. We can go out to the Great Place and visit him."

Ramose smiled at Karoya, remembering the time he, Karoya and Hapu, the apprentice painter, had all lived and worked in the desert valley which Ramose's father had chosen as the place to build his tomb. Without the help and friendship of Karoya and Hapu, Ramose would never have survived his exile.

"We can take Pegget," said Ramose. "He's never been to the Great Place."

"We can visit your tomb," said Karoya smiling. "Leave offerings for your spirit."

"My tomb is empty again," said Ramose. "They have taken the mummy of the young boy who was buried in my place and interred him in his own tomb."

They disturbed a flock of ibis, wading in the mud by the river's edge. The birds took off in front of them.

"Things must be bad in Kush," Ramose said, "if Vizier Wersu thinks we have to take hostages."

"He's Pharaoh's guest, remember," Karoya said with a wry smile. "Not a prisoner."

"He's a hostage," replied Ramose. "Vizier Wersu would have threatened the rebel leader with the death of his son if he attacks more Egyptian settlements."

"It's better than waging war on my people."

"Does he have a name, this rebel prince?"

"His name is Kashta."

"What is he like?" asked Ramose.

"He's angry," replied Karoya.

Ramose nodded. "I imagine he's furious. I would be if someone took me hostage."

The friends walked back to the palace. It was time for the evening meal. Ramose brightened. He was happy to be close to his brother, and seeing Karoya again had been a welcome surprise—the food was very good too.

Ramose was up early the following morning.

"I'm going to visit our guest from Kush," he said to Karoya. "Pegget is keen to meet him. Will you come and translate?"

Karoya nodded. "You won't find him willing to talk."

Ramose shrugged. "My brother is king of all Egypt. I can't argue with him."

The palace didn't have a prison. It had been built before the days when Egypt was fighting with its neighbours. The rebel had been placed in a small but comfortable room in a wing of the palace where senior servants lived. Two armed guards stood at the door.

"Pharaoh would like to speak to the prisoner," Ramose told them.

The guards bowed as the young pharaoh approached. One of them hurried to unlock the door.

"Karoya and I will talk to him first," Ramose told his brother.

The room was plain and simply furnished with a bed and a chair. Sunlight filtered through grilles high in the walls, lighting worn patterns painted on the floor.

A dark face glowered at Ramose as he entered the room. Ramose studied the Kushite rebel. He was a young man, not much older than Ramose himself. He was dressed in a clean Egyptian kilt, but he had thick gold rings in his ears. His skin was like Karoya's, a deep, dark brown like polished wood. His hair was like hers as well, twisting in tight curls all over his head. That was where the similarity with Karoya ended. Where Karoya's face was more often than not split with a wide smile, Kashta's mouth was grim and unsmiling.

"Tell him who I am and that Pharaoh wishes to speak to him," Ramose said to Karoya.

Karoya spoke to the rebel in her own language. He spat some words back at Karoya.

"He doesn't want to speak to any Egyptian, especially Pharaoh," she translated.

"Tell him—"

The prisoner picked up a plate of food and hurled it towards them with more angry words.

"It seems he's not in the mood for visitors," said Tuthmosis when he saw Ramose come out of the room wiping lentil stew from his kilt.

"No. Perhaps we could go fishing instead," said Ramose.

One of Hatshepsut's women suddenly appeared in the corridor.

"Princess Hatshepsut requires Prince Ramose's presence in the western hall," she announced.

"Tell your mistress that I'm busy," said Ramose.

"Her highness was definite that she wanted you to attend. Immediately," the woman said.

Ramose was annoyed that his sister thought that she could summon him like a slave or a pet dog, but the woman didn't look like she was going to move out of Ramose's way until he followed her. Ramose reluctantly made his way to the western hall.

Hatshepsut was sitting on her favourite chair—the one with the high back and the arm-rests carved in the shape of jackals. The gold and precious stones inlaid in it glittered in the rays of sun that entered through the high windows. Her women companions were with her as always, but they were sitting to one side.

Hatshepsut was surrounded instead by the palace ministers and two generals of Pharaoh's army.

The men were all listening carefully as she pointed to a map spread out on a table before her. Ramose couldn't quite hear what she was saying, but she seemed to be making suggestions about sending troops to Libya to control an uprising there. She finished speaking before Ramose was close enough to hear clearly.

"Thank you, gentlemen," she said.

The ministers and generals all bowed and started to back out of the hall.

"I'd like you all to stay," she said. "There is a matter I want to discuss with Prince Ramose."

Ramose had noticed that Hatshepsut never referred to him as her brother anymore.

"A message has arrived from one of the generals who is campaigning in the land of Naharin." She paused to take a sip of wine from a golden goblet. "Despite my father's military success in this land, there is unrest."

"That's because we keep forcing Naharini men to join the Egyptian army and sending them away from their homes," said Ramose. He had been in Naharin, a country on the edge of the

Great Green Sea far to the north of Egypt, six months earlier.

"The barbarians beyond Egypt's borders must learn to kneel before Pharaoh."

"The people of Naharin are not barbarians," Ramose said angrily. "I spent several weeks there discussing everything from grape cultivation to poetry with one of their leaders."

"They have attacked our garrisons."

"They are proud people who don't want to be ruled by foreigners."

"So you would prefer a diplomatic settlement with these people?" Hatshepsut said picking a thread from her gown. "Rather than an armed attack on them?"

"Of course," replied Ramose. "I'm in favour of any course of action than would avoid bloodshed."

The corners of Hatshepsut's mouth curved up slightly. It was the closest she ever got to smiling. Ramose had no idea what she was about to say, but he had a feeling he wasn't going to like it.

"I'm glad Prince Ramose is so fond of the people of Naharin," she said in a voice like snake venom mixed with honey. "I am proposing an alliance with Naharin. A marriage," Hatshepsut paused as she took a fig from one of her women. "A marriage between Princess Tiya, youngest daughter of the ruler of Naharin, and Pharaoh's brother, Prince Ramose."

Ramose's mouth dropped open. He couldn't believe what he was hearing.

"Marriage?" was all he managed to say.

3

ENSNARED

"YOU should be pleased," said Hatshepsut, still smiling spitefully. "This solution doesn't involve bloodshed. None of your friends in Naharin need die. It's a peaceful solution, just as you wanted. You, of course, will be required to live in Naharin with your wife, to ensure that your new relatives behave themselves."

Ramose could feel anger surging up inside him. Hatshepsut had baited a hook and he had obediently swallowed it. All of the things Hatshepsut had done to him before—lying to him, imprisoning him, betraying him—had made him more sad than angry. This made him furious. Hatshepsut wanted him out of the way. Ramose realised that his sister had ambitions. Tuthmosis might be pharaoh, but Hatshepsut wanted to be in control—not just of the palace but of all Egypt.

"You have no right to tell me what to do!" shouted Ramose. "I won't marry a barbarian princess."

Hatshepsut smiled triumphantly. "I didn't think you thought of our neighbours as barbarians, Ramose," she said. "I thought you believed they were all equal in status to Egyptians."

Ramose was furious with himself that he'd made such a slip. It only made Hatshepsut gloat even more.

He was about to storm out of the hall, when Vizier Wersu entered.

"Vizier," said Ramose. "I'm glad you're here. Hatshepsut has—"

"I have already spoken to Vizier Wersu," said Hatshepsut.

She turned to the vizier. "Have you considered my proposal?"

"I have, Highness."

The vizier looked at Ramose uncomfortably. "I have had only a day or two to contemplate the matter."

"It isn't something that requires a lot of thought, Wersu," snapped Hatshepsut. "You either think it is a good plan or not."

The vizier didn't speak straightaway. He looked at Hatshepsut. He looked at Ramose and then at the floor.

"I have to agree with Princess Hatshepsut. An alliance like this would solve our problems in Naharin."

Ramose was horrified. "But I don't want to marry anybody, especially someone I've never even met."

"Actually you have met her," said Hatshepsut. "She was in the royal residence when you visited Naharin last year. She was presented to you."

Ramose bit his lip. He would have to learn not to argue with Hatshepsut. The more he wriggled the deeper the hook went in.

"How do you—?"

There was no point in asking. Hatshepsut had her spies everywhere. He glared at the vizier.

"I'm glad we agree on this matter, Wersu," said Hatshepsut. She didn't smile, but there was a look of satisfaction in her eyes. "We'll speak further on the matter."

She stood up ready to leave.

"Oh, I almost forgot, Vizier," she said. The corners of her mouth turned up and Ramose knew the vizier was about to become the next victim of Hatshepsut's spite. "If you're looking for your 'hostage', I have ordered that he be removed from the pleasant quarters you assigned him and put somewhere more suitable for an enemy of Egypt." Then she left the hall.

"I'm sorry, Excellency," said the vizier. "I know that this is something that you don't want to do."

"She wants to get rid of me and you're helping her. Why do you side with her, even though she overrules you?"

"My job is to serve Egypt," replied the vizier sternly. "You have heard the news of an uprising in Libya. We are now fighting on three fronts. The army is spread thin. We are training new recruits, but that will take time. Such a marriage would put an immediate end to one conflict."

Ramose wasn't convinced. "You're under her spell just like the ministers. I'm the only one who's willing to stand up to her."

"I am completely aware that the princess's main reason for this scheme is to have you out of the way."

"So why are you supporting her?"

"It is good for Egypt. If one of these rebellions can be settled without sending an army, we can concentrate our armed forces in Libya and Kush."

"I won't do it."

"If there was any other way…"

"I want to be here in the palace at Pharaoh's side."

"Egypt is not invincible. It is your duty to do what's best for Egypt, Ramose. Just as it is mine." The vizier gently put his bony hand on Ramose's shoulder. It was the first time he'd called him by his name. "I'm sorry, but we must all do what we can to avert war."

Ramose paced about his chamber. He felt like a caged animal, like a leopard on a leash. Karoya came into his room and sat on the bed without saying anything.

"You've heard?" asked Ramose.

"Vizier Wersu told me. He said you were angry."

"I'm not angry," said Ramose. "I'm furious." He kicked a sandal out of his way.

"Would you like to go for a walk by the river?" asked Karoya.

"I'm not going to spend the rest of my life doing her bidding," he said, ignoring Karoya.

"Perhaps Pharaoh is free to go fishing."

Karoya could usually improve Ramose's bad moods and distract him from an annoyance, but she had never known him to be so angry before.

"She wants to rule Egypt herself," Ramose said. "I didn't believe it at first, but now I'm convinced."

Ramose's pacing brought him up against one of the painted walls. He slapped his hands against it, as if he wished to pace right through it.

"Everyone is frightened of her. Even Wersu."

"The vizier only wants what's best for Egypt," said Karoya.

Ramose whipped round to face her.

"So you're siding with them now!"

"I'm not. I just—"

"Just because she gave you a bracelet once when you were still a slave, doesn't mean you have to stand up for her forever."

"Ramose, I'm not—"

"Everybody's turned on me. I thought I could at least rely on you."

Ramose brushed past Karoya and stormed out of the room. There was no one left he could talk to. His friends were mesmerised by Hatshepsut. She had them all in the palm of her hand. Ramose wasn't going to jump to her commands. He would be the one person to defy her. He stamped down the corridors, knocking a basket of figs out of the arms of a servant. He had to get back at Hatshepsut, show her she wasn't going to rule his life.

It took Ramose quite a while to discover where his sister had put Kashta, the rebel prisoner. The palace had been built with pleasure and comfort in mind. Even the servants' quarters were bright and pleasant. Hatshepsut's dedication was admirable. She had managed to find the darkest and most unpleasant room in the whole palace. It was a storeroom next to the stables.

"I want to see the prisoner," said Ramose to the two armed guards standing in front of the door. Where did they get such big men from? he thought, looking up at the guards towering above him.

"Her Highness Princess Hatshepsut has said that the prisoner is not allowed to have visitors," one of the guards said.

Ramose had thought this might happen. "I have a note from her," he said, producing a scrap of papyrus with a few words scribbled on it. It was actually a recipe for ibis stew that he'd picked up on his way through the kitchens. He'd rubbed lotus petals on it to make it smell as if it had come from his sister. He hoped the guards didn't notice the cooking oil stains on it. The two big men peered at the note but, as Ramose had gambled, neither of them could read a word of it.

"Her Highness wants the prisoner to be exercised. She doesn't want him taking sick," lied Ramose. "A dead hostage isn't much use," he added cheerfully.

The guards reluctantly unbarred the door and Ramose entered.

It was dark and smelly inside. It took Ramose's eyes a few moments to become accustomed to the dim light. There was no window and no furniture. Kashta was sitting on a scatter of straw on the floor. He blinked in the glare of light coming from the open door.

"I thought you might be more in the mood for a visitor this time," said Ramose smiling down at the prisoner. "I might even try and find you some better quarters. You have to promise not to throw food at me though."

Kashta looked at Ramose blankly. Ramose pulled the prisoner to his feet.

"Now if you behave yourself, I'll take you for a walk," Ramose said. He mimed walking with his fingers.

"I would like that," said Kashta.

Ramose looked at him in surprise. "I thought you couldn't speak Egyptian."

"Egyptians have been ruling my country for five years," the prisoner replied. "I would have been stupid not to learn it."

"Give me your word that you won't try and escape, and we can go for a walk around the palace grounds."

"You have my word," said Kashta.

"I'll bind your hands," said Ramose. "Just to keep the guards happy. We don't want them running off to tell my sister."

Ramose loosely bound Kashta's hands with a length of rope. The guards watched as their prisoner strolled off down the corridor. Ramose took him out into the gardens. There was nobody around.

Kashta looked happier than he had the last time Ramose had seen him. He breathed in the fresh air appreciatively and turned his dark face towards the sun. The sour look on his face gradually changed to a smile.

"Everybody is resting after the midday meal," Ramose explained. "I'll show you the lotus pool first."

Ramose awoke. It was dark. "It must be the middle of the night," he thought. His head hurt. In fact, it felt like it was about to split in two. His bed felt unusually hard. He turned over. Or at least he tried to. He couldn't move. He was wedged up against something and his arms wouldn't move from where they were—both behind his back.

His cheek hurt too as if he'd bashed it on something. He tried to sit up and banged his head. He groaned with the pain. Why did his head hurt so? Slowly he realised that he wasn't in his bed. He was lying on his side with his knees doubled up and he couldn't straighten them. He was inside something—inside something small. It wasn't

night time either. A thin line of light was seeping
in from outside whatever it was he was locked in.

Like a bad dream, it all started to come back to
him. He remembered taking Kashta out into the
gardens and how pleased he'd been that the
Kushite prince was so interested in the plants.
He remembered how Kashta had asked all sorts
of questions. How he'd apologised for his previous
bad behaviour. Ramose had chattered on about
all the things he'd learned in foreign lands.

Kashta was interested in everything he said,
especially all the tools and devices Ramose had
learned about abroad. He wanted to see the
papyrus with the list of useful foreign things.
Kashta said he could only read a little, but with
Ramose's help he'd be able to understand it.
Ramose had taken him to his chamber, thinking
it would be good to have a friend in the palace,
since everyone else had turned against him.
Kashta had admired the wall paintings and the
courtyard. Ramose had got out the papyrus from
his elegantly carved chest and laid it on the
bed...that was the last he remembered.

It was all his own fault. Ramose couldn't
imagine how he'd been so stupid. He could hardly
bear to think about it. He remembered Kashta's
polite conversation, his courteous thanks for a fig
picked from a tree, his interest in Ramose's travels. His face burned when he remembered how

the Kushite rebel had been so charming and friendly. Ramose had fallen for it, like a pigeon following a trail of wheat grains into a trap. He knew where he was now. He was inside his own chest. Kashta must have hit him on the head with something, knocked him out and locked him in the chest.

Ramose's anger and humiliation suddenly gave way to panic. He was locked in a box. He hated confined spaces. His hands were tied behind his back. He couldn't move. He could hardly breathe. He pushed against the lid with his feet. It didn't shift. The lack of air and blackness was stifling. His breaths were coming short and fast. He shouted out for help. He kicked and wriggled and screamed. Surely someone would hear him. He shouted until he was hoarse. All he'd done was use up the air inside the chest. His head was spinning.

He tried to focus his thoughts. Eventually someone would come into the chamber. Karoya would come looking for him or a servant would come to see why he hadn't turned up for the evening meal. When it was discovered that Kashta was missing, Hatshepsut would guess it was his doing. She'd more than likely send a guard to arrest him. He might not hear them though. He couldn't keep banging and shouting, he'd just exhaust himself and the air in the chest.

He pictured the outside of the chest. It was kept closed by slipping a short wooden peg through four wooden rings, two on the lid, two on the chest itself. When the lid was closed the rings lined up and the peg slid through them all. It was not a strong mechanism. It was meant to keep out mice not thieves. It certainly wasn't designed to keep prisoners in. It would be skillfully made though, like all Egyptian things. It wouldn't break easily.

Tied up the way he was, there was only one thing he could do. He had to try and tip the chest over. If it fell forwards there was a slim chance that the catch might break. If it didn't, at least when servants came into the chamber they would set the chest upright. If he was awake he could call out. If he was unconscious, the unusual weight of the chest would make them open it.

Ramose wriggled until he was lying on his back with his doubled-up knees above him. He rocked from side to side in the enclosed space. Slowly at first and then with gathering speed and force, he flung himself against first one side of the chest and then the other. The chest was squat and solid but it was supported on four slender legs, beautifully carved like most of the palace furniture and ending in animals' feet.

As he rocked, he pictured the delicate feline feet with the claws gilded with gold paint. He felt the chest lift slightly. He threw himself harder, ignoring the pain. The chest started to rock with him. Which way would it fall? He threw himself to the front of the chest with the last of his energy and the chest crashed to the floor.

Ramose hoped that the combined weight of the box and his body on the wooden catch had smashed it. He pushed with his knees and the lid moved. He pushed again and rolled out onto the floor. He breathed in greedy mouthfuls of fresh air and slowly stretched out his aching legs. He was free, but his ordeal wasn't over yet. Now he had to face the vizier and his sister.

His hands were still tied tightly behind his back and his legs were aching and stinging as his blood started to circulate again. He crawled to the door and managed to get to his knees and then to his tingling feet. He grasped the door handle with his tied hands and managed to open the door. He tried to walk but his legs wouldn't obey him. He stumbled and fell at the feet of a startled servant.

Ramose sat slumped in a chair in Pharaoh's audience hall. The palace physician bathed the cut on his head where Kashta had knocked him out with his own hawk-headed statue of Ra. The physician spread salve on his many bruises. A priest recited healing prayers and hung amulets around his neck.

"I'm all right," he said, pushing them both away.

"You don't look all right, Ramose," said Tuthmosis, who was peering at him with a worried look.

There was a ring of people staring at him: his brother, his sister, the vizier, several ministers. They weren't all wearing a worried frown like his brother, though. The vizier was thin-lipped and angry.

"You've ruined Vizier Wersu's plan to keep the Kushite rebels under control," Hatshepsut said with more pleasure than disappointment.

Ramose wasn't in the mood for lectures, especially from his sister.

"It wasn't very nice of Kashta to knock you on the head and lock you in a chest," said Tuthmosis.

Ramose knew he was trying to be helpful, but he could do without the sort of help that pointed out how stupid he'd been.

"And it certainly wasn't nice of him to take Karoya."

Ramose sat up. "What did you say?"

"Karoya is missing," said the vizier. "She hasn't been seen since this morning."

"She more than likely helped him escape and has gone to join the rebels," said Hatshepsut. "You can't trust barbarians."

Ramose glared at his sister. "She would never do such a thing."

"Did she leave a note?" asked Tuthmosis.

Ramose jumped to his feet and hurried to Karoya's room, followed by the vizier, Tuthmosis and several anxious servants. Her belongings were still neatly placed around the room: her pen box, her woven reed fan and an alabaster statue of a cat that Ramose had given her.

"She would never leave these things behind," Ramose said. "Kashta's kidnapped her."

The vizier didn't look so sure. "We can't be certain—"

"I have to go to Kush," said Ramose, hurrying towards the door as if he intended to leave immediately. "I have to find Karoya."

4

OUT OF EGYPT

NOBODY wanted Ramose to go in search of
Karoya. Vizier Wersu thought it was too
dangerous. Tuthmosis complained about
his brother leaving the palace so soon.
Hatshepsut was concerned that he would not be
back in time for the arrival of the Naharini
princess. It took Ramose two weeks to convince
everybody that he should go. Hatshepsut was the

hardest to persuade. In the end, he agreed to marry the foreign princess when he returned.

By the time he was ready to leave, it was the beginning of akhet, the season of the inundation. Each year as summer came, the waters of the Nile started to flow faster. The river grew deeper and wider until all the surrounding farmland was flooded with dark green water. This was Ra's gift to Egypt. When the floodwaters receded in autumn, they would leave behind a layer of black silt, rich in the goodness that would make the crops flourish.

Usually, boats travelling south simply hoisted a sail and were carried along by the prevailing wind. At the time of the inundation, however, the flow of the river was strong and erratic as it surged towards the sea. Teams of rowers had to work hard to keep the boats from being carried by the side currents and running aground on the submerged fields.

Because of the inundation, there were no trade boats sailing south, but boats full of soldiers were making their way to Kush to quash the Kushite rebels. Ramose got permission to travel on one of these boats.

It was a sturdy craft made of cedar wood, carrying a company of soldiers to defend the fortress town of Sai. The boat was crowded with new recruits who looked like they had all been chosen for the enormous size of their muscled arms and legs.

Ramose was glad to be sailing away from the palace. The oarsmen grunted with the strain of their work, but the landscape only slipped by slowly. It was going to take weeks to get to Kush. He wondered where Karoya was now. He wished he hadn't spoken so harshly to her the last time he had seen her.

When Ramose had made his previous journey to Kush, he'd had Karoya as company. She didn't like being on the river and she had chattered constantly to keep her mind off the deep waters surrounding her, telling him about her country and her people. Ramose had taught her to read and write Egyptian. She was a clever girl, eager to learn and by the time they'd reached Kush, she had mastered the skills. This journey would be different. The soldiers didn't even glance in his direction, let alone talk to him.

The boat slowed as the first shift of rowers stopped to rest and another crew took over. The weary rowers all filed to the stern where they were given bread, fruit and beer. One soldier seemed to be particularly hungry. He was piling up more bread and figs after the others had all returned to their benches. Sweat was still glistening on his huge arms and legs. Sensing that someone was watching him, the soldier looked up at Ramose who was wedged between sacks of grain at the back of the boat. The soldier suddenly dropped his food and launched himself at Ramose. Ramose flinched, thinking that the huge soldier was about to attack him. Instead he found himself being swallowed up in a crushing hug.

"Don't you talk to your old friends now that everyone knows you're a prince?" asked the young soldier in a deep voice.

Ramose pulled himself away and peered at the smiling, sweaty face. It would have been an attractive face if not for the nose, which was pushed to one side as if it had once been broken.

"Hapu?" Ramose said. "Is that you?" Ramose couldn't believe that this bulky soldier was his old friend. "You must have grown nearly a cubit! I though you were working at the Great Place."

Hapu sat down beside Ramose.

"I finished my apprenticeship, but I didn't get on with the painters. They'd all heard that I was a friend of Prince Ramose. I didn't act any different, I know I didn't, but they decided I was stuck up. They said I was too big for my sandals. When one of the generals came to the Great Place to conscript boys into the army, they put my name down." Hapu shrugged his broad shoulders. "I didn't really mind. I wasn't happy there."

"You look so different," said Ramose, peering at Hapu and trying to find his skinny little friend in the muscled soldier with the deep voice sitting next to him. "I didn't even recognise you."

"It's me," said Hapu as he took an enormous mouthful of bread and thumped Ramose on the back. "Where are you going? Down to the palace at Pathyris?"

"Further than that. I'm going to Kush, just like you."

"That's good. We'll have plenty of time together. It's two hours before my next shift at the oars. Tell me everything that you've been doing since I saw you last."

Ramose didn't know where to begin. There was so much to tell. He'd had two years of adventures in foreign lands. He'd have plenty of time to tell Hapu about that later. Instead he started at the end of his story.

"I'd been looking forward to returning to the palace so much," he told Hapu. "I enjoyed travelling the world, and I'd had some wonderful adventures, but I was ready to go home. Nothing turned out the way I thought it would, though."

Ramose told Hapu how he'd imagined he would become Pharaoh's chief adviser when he got home. He knew Tuthmosis looked up to his big brother and thought he would do anything he suggested. Ramose hadn't counted on the ministers and the servants who never left him alone for a minute.

"In the time that I was home," Ramose explained, "I only managed to talk to my brother in private twice—and both times we had to sneak away like thieves."

"How is Pharaoh, may he have long life, health and prosperity?"

"He's well enough, I suppose, but he's not happy. It's a lonely life for a boy his age."

"And your sister?" asked Hapu tentatively.

"I was hoping that we'd be able to settle our differences," Ramose sighed. "Without you and Karoya to keep me company, I needed a friend. I'd thought that Hatshepsut and I could be friends again, like we used to be."

Ramose went quiet. Hapu let his friend tell him in his own time.

"That wasn't the way it turned out though. Hatshepsut is even more cold and distant." Ramose glanced around to make sure no one was listening. "I haven't mentioned this to anyone in the palace, Hapu, but I think she wants to take control of Egypt herself."

"That's not possible!" exclaimed Hapu, spitting out breadcrumbs. "In all the history of Egypt, going back hundreds and hundreds of years, there's never been a woman ruling the two lands. Either you're going crazy or she is!"

"You haven't heard anything yet," said Ramose, lowering his voice.

"She has a plan to get rid of me."

Hapu looked worried. "You don't mean…"

"No, she's not trying to kill me. This is worse. She wants to marry me to a Naharini princess."

"Marriage? You?" said Hapu, laughing out loud.

Some of the soldiers turned round to see what was going on.

"That's what I said," replied Ramose quietly. "Except I didn't find it funny. She's serious. And Vizier Wersu agreed with her."

"So that's why you're running away from the palace," said Hapu. "You don't want to marry a barbarian princess."

"I don't want to marry anybody," replied Ramose, "but there's something else I haven't told you. Something more worrying than any of that. I've been chattering on for an hour, moaning about my problems and I haven't even told you about Karoya."

As the Nile made its way towards Thebes from its mysterious beginnings in some unknown place far to the south, its course was disturbed in six different places. At these six points, known as the cataracts, the smooth stream of the river was suddenly turned into a confused jumble as it cascaded over rocks. The boat reached the first cataract in ten days. With the river swollen by floodwaters, the rocks were below the surface but they still created rapids. Every soldier on board had to man the oars, two or three to each oar. Even Ramose had to lend a hand.

The commander, a man much smaller than his troop of soldiers, shouted orders until he was hoarse, guiding the rowers through the treacherous waters. Several times the boat was caught in strong side currents that threatened to overturn it, but the soldiers managed to force it back to the central stream.

Whenever Hapu wasn't rowing, doing exercises or learning military strategies, he came and sat with Ramose.

"Are you sure that Karoya was kidnapped by Kashta?" Hapu asked.

"Of course. What else could have happened?" replied Ramose, thinking of his last angry words to Karoya.

"I don't know," said Hapu. "She probably didn't like the formality of life in the palace."

Ramose didn't say anything.

"Perhaps she just needed to get back to the desert," continued Hapu. "It must have been hard with her people at war with Egypt. Whoever she sided with she would have felt like a traitor."

Ramose remained silent.

"But, you're right, she wouldn't have gone off to become a desert nomad without a word to you, would she?"

Ramose finally spoke. "There's one thing I haven't told you."

Hapu looked at his friend. "What?"

"The last time I saw Karoya, we had an argument. At least, I was arguing. I didn't give her a chance to say much at all."

Ramose remembered his harsh words. "I was furious because Hatshepsut had set me up. I accused Karoya of siding with Hatshepsut."

"She'd never do that."

"I know. I was angry. I just took it out on her. That was the last time I saw her."

"So you think she may have been running away from you?"

"I don't know. It's possible. I have to find out, to make sure she's not in any danger."

Ramose looked out over the expanse of water surrounding them.

"How long does your commander think it will be before we arrive in Kush?" he asked.

"He doesn't expect to reach Sai for another three weeks at least."

Just over a week later, they reached the fortress town of Buhen. They were now far from the safety of Thebes, deep within the newly conquered territories of Egypt. The occupants of Buhen lived in the shadow of a fort, built to protect the Egyptians who lived there and to remind anyone who thought about attacking the town of the strength of the conquerors. Instead of the usual simple wooden wharves where boats were tied up, there were large stone quays. The fort wasn't only there to protect people. Buhen was also a storehouse where goods from Kush, collected as taxes, were stored ready to be sent north to Egypt. It also acted as a supply depot where food and equipment for Egyptian forts further up the Nile were stockpiled.

"I hope I have some time to look around after we've finished taking on supplies," said Hapu excitedly. Although he had travelled more than the average Egyptian, this was the first large town that he had been to other than Thebes. Even though Buhen had been part of Egypt for a number of years, it still had the atmosphere of a foreign place.

Ramose was relieved to be off the boat. Glad to have a chance to stretch his legs. He was also keen to find out if anyone had seen Kashta and Karoya.

Beyond the quays was the fort. It was a massive building, as big as the palace in Thebes. The palace had been built to please the eye. Its walls were whitewashed, its shape elegant. The fort was made of plain unadorned mud bricks. Its huge walls formed a large, squat square and were punctured at regular intervals with rectangular holes, just large enough for a bowman to take aim through. The walls were topped with triangular shaped battlements, which allowed lookouts and bowmen to look down over the surrounding country but still have some protection. They gave the fort a threatening look, as if it was topped by a row of sharp teeth.

"Look at the defences," said Hapu, staring as they passed through a gateway in a high mound of rammed earth. They crossed a bridge over a trench twelve cubits deep and then stood in the shadow of a high mud brick wall. They passed through another gateway, but they still weren't inside the fort.

"There's another wall," Hapu said, gaping at the massive inner wall. "It's even higher. It must be twenty-five cubits high and ten cubits wide."

Lookouts were walking around on top of the wall, armed with bows and spears. At each gate they were questioned by guards. Inside, there was a large area where the soldiers trained. Neat rows of low mud brick buildings were dwarfed by the towering walls. This was where the fort's soldiers lived. There were also administrative buildings, storehouses, workshops and stables. The fort contained everything the garrison needed to survive if it was besieged. All the buildings were stark and plain. There were no carvings on the walls, no statues.

Hapu's battalion had to collect supplies from the stores for their journey south.

"I'll see you after we've finished," Hapu said and ran off to join the other soldiers.

Ramose knew that Kashta would have passed through Buhen on his way to Kush. He hoped he might find out if Karoya had been with him.

The port administrator's office was an unimposing building made of plain mud brick like everything else.

Inside a scribe was scribbling lists of goods arriving from the south.

"I'd like an audience with the administrator," said Ramose.

"Have you been appointed a time to meet with him?" asked the scribe, without stopping writing.

"No. I've only just arrived from Thebes."

"He will be able to see you in four days."

"I won't be here in four days," said Ramose. "I'm here as Pharaoh's representative," Ramose held out his medallion, wishing he'd taken the time to get the missing jewels replaced and the inscription recarved.

"The administrator is not in Buhen. Even Pharaoh himself—may he have long life, health and prosperity—would not be able to get an audience with him."

The scribe put down his pen with an impatient sigh. "Perhaps I can be of assistance."

Ramose got the impression that the scribe wasn't at all interested in assisting him.

"I'm looking for two people who passed through Buhen two weeks ago."

"Hundreds of people pass through Buhen each week," said the scribe irritably. "How can I be expected to remember two in particular?"

"These two are from Kush."

"I certainly can't be expected to remember two slaves."

"They aren't slaves. They would be travelling alone. One may have been travelling as Pharaoh's Chief Envoy in Kush."

"May have?" said the scribe suspiciously.

"She may not have shown her papers."

"I'm sure I would have remembered two people from Kush travelling alone."

Ramose made similar inquiries at the offices of the battalion commander and the storekeeper. The response was the same. When Ramose had asked everyone he could think of, he sat down in the shade of the huge walls.

"There you are," said Hapu. "I've been looking everywhere for you. Did you have any luck?"

"No," replied Ramose. "No one has seen them. It doesn't make sense."

"Well, there's nothing more you can do. I've finished my duties. We have an hour before we have to report back to the boat. Let's look around."

"I've looked around already."

"Do you think you could get us into the store-house?"

"Haven't you just been in the storehouses collecting supplies?"

"I don't mean those storehouses. I mean the one full of foreign treasure and strange creatures," said Hapu excitedly.

Ramose had other things on his mind, but he remembered his own excitement the first time he had been to Buhen. "My authority doesn't seem to have impressed anyone so far, but I'll see what I can do."

Ramose showed the guards the papyrus which proclaimed that he was Superintendent of Foreign Lands and they were allowed to go into the storehouse. It was full of chests of gold rings, stacks of ebony and cedar, piles of elephant tusks. There were ostrich feathers and leopard skins all ready to be shipped to Thebes.

"These are the taxes that the people of Kush have to pay for the privilege of being defeated by Egypt," said Ramose.

Behind the storehouses, there was an enclosure where live animals were kept: the baboons and leopards that Egyptians were so fond of. Hapu stopped dead in his tracks.

"What's that creature?" he said, staring up at a bizarre animal. "It's as tall as an obelisk."

He stared at the animal's long neck, its spindly legs and its strange skin: yellow with irregular brown patches.

"It's a giraffe," said Ramose.

"What is it used for?" asked Hapu. "Is it good to eat?"

"It has no special use that I know of. The local people use the skin for making clothing."

"So why is it being sent to Egypt?"

"Just as a curiosity," replied Ramose. "Something to amuse the children of palace officials."

Outside the storehouse an enterprising young man had set up a stall. He was selling trinkets from foreign lands: jewellery made of shells and animals' teeth, little pouches made of animal skin. Ramose wouldn't have even noticed the stall, but it was meant to attract people like Hapu who were travelling outside of Egypt for the first time.

"Look, Ramose," he said. "There's a pouch made of giraffe skin. I could keep my gold ring and copper in it."

"You won't have any gold or copper left if you waste it on trifles everywhere you go."

Hapu wouldn't be dissuaded though. He was like an excited child. He bought his giraffe skin pouch and the seller was trying hard to make him buy a necklace as well. Something on the stall suddenly caught Ramose's eye. It was a bracelet. It didn't come from the lands south of Egypt though. It came from Kadesh to Egypt's north.

"Hapu," he said, grabbing his friend's arm. "Look at this bracelet."

"It's very pretty," said Hapu, "but I don't want a bracelet."

"It's Karoya's," said Ramose. "It was a present I bought for her."

Ramose turned to the trinket seller.

"Where did you get this bracelet? Who sold it to you?"

The stallholder wouldn't say anything until Ramose bought the bracelet. He paid a lot more than it was worth, which loosened the boy's tongue. He remembered the girl who sold it. She was from Kush but well-dressed like an Egyptian.

Ramose hurried back to the boat eager to get on with the voyage.

"We still don't know where she is," said Hapu.

"No, but we know that she came this way."

5

IN THE HANDS
OF RA

THREE DAYS later, they reached the second cataract. The rapids there were even more treacherous than they had been at the first cataract. The waters of the inundation were so strong that year that huge boulders had been forced from their beds and washed downstream. The swollen river cascaded over the newly arranged rocks in an angry turmoil. There was nowhere for a boat to pass safely. The commander ordered the soldiers to row to the shore. They had no choice but to drag the big boat onto the muddy bank and then pull it on a sled over land until they were past the treacherous cataract.

Ramose made the mistake of suggesting an easier route than the rocky path that was close to the river that the commander had chosen. The soldiers had hesitated, unsure of who to obey. The commander shouted at them even louder than usual until they obeyed him.

It took three days of backbreaking work to get the boat around the cataract, but the commander would not allow the exhausted soldiers to rest. Ramose tried to protest. The commander only ever shouted at his men, and his voice seemed unnaturally polite when he told Ramose that he wanted to keep moving.

Ramose had often caught the commander watching him suspiciously. He was sure that Hatshepsut had paid the commander to keep an eye on him and make sure he didn't leave the boat. No doubt when they reached Sai, others would be paid to watch him.

The soldiers still kept their distance from the strange brother of Pharaoh. Ramose had tried to be friendly and help whenever he could, but having a prince bring them water when they were at the oars only seemed to make them more uncomfortable. If it hadn't been for Hapu's company, Ramose thought he would have gone mad from boredom.

"Another week and we should be in sight of Sai," said Hapu.

They had just had a brief stop in the town of Semna. There was a fort at Semna similar to the one at Buhen, probably similar to the one in Sai. The land as far as the sixth cataract had all been conquered and was all part of Egypt, but the people who lived in these lands didn't think of themselves as Egyptians. All along the river in these southern lands there were fortresses built to protect the conquerors from possible uprisings.

"Look at that," said Hapu through a mouthful of fruit.

They were just south of Semna. Hapu was pointing to the western bank of the river where a new temple was being built. Instead of being built out of blocks of stone, brought from a distant quarry, it was being chiselled straight out of the natural rock that rose from the river on both sides. Steps led up from the river to four enormous statues of Pharaoh sitting with his hands on his knees. Sculptors were working on one statue as they passed, chipping off pieces of white rock with chisels to turn the shapeless rock into a royal hand. Others below were concentrating on the detail of the Pharaoh's toenails. A shapeless piece of rock was where the head would be. The other three statues were closer to completion. They all had blank faces staring peacefully in front of them. None of the faces looked anything like his brother.

Hapu went back to eating his midday meal. Ramose was still amazed at the amount his friend ate at every meal. He'd already eaten three loaves, six fish and a dozen figs and he still wasn't full. He was looking at the half loaf that Ramose had left in his bowl.

"If you're not going to eat that…" he said.

"Take it," replied Ramose. "I couldn't possibly eat another thing."

Hapu took the bread. "I have to build my strength," he said, stuffing it into his mouth. "Ready for my next shift at the oars."

The farmland grew sparser and the villages grew smaller. On either side of the Nile, the strip of fertile land was so narrow that the desert beyond was visible from the river. This land was wild and untilled. Trees and bushes grew wherever they chose. There were no farmers pausing during their work to watch them pass, no cattle grazing. Flocks of ibis and heron flew overhead and then settled to wade along the muddy banks looking for worms. If anyone lived in the wilderness, they kept themselves hidden.

Hapu was unsettled by the wild land. He had

never seen fertile land that hadn't been tamed by the plough for the purpose of growing crops. It seemed strange that this land, capable of growing food for many people, lay unused. Ramose remembered having a similar feeling when he had first travelled that way.

"Could Karoya have gone to visit her family?" Hapu asked, breaking the silence.

"She has no family," said Ramose sadly. "They were all killed more than two years ago."

Hapu looked uncomfortable. "By Egyptian soldiers?"

Ramose nodded grimly. "She has only one relative left. Her mother's sister who has married into another tribe."

"Where is she?"

"She lives in a small village east of Tombos."

"You couldn't blame Karoya if she didn't want to live among Egyptians," said Hapu. "And you know how she loves the desert. I think the most likely thing is that she's joined a nomad tribe."

Ramose knew that if Karoya wanted to go back to her nomadic life and never see an Egyptian again, not even him, there was nothing he could do about it.

"But what if you're wrong?" he said. "What if Kashta did kidnap her and she's in danger?"

Hapu shrugged his shoulders. "Then you have to find her."

There was an eerie silence. The landscape had changed again. On either side of the river, barren, rocky land rose up to bleak hills. There were few pockets of earth where plants could grow. All Ramose could hear was the rush of the river and the occasional screech of monkeys. Ramose knew that this empty land was where the Kushite rebels hid.

It was hot, hotter than it ever got in Thebes. The soldiers, tired as they were, were rowing hard. They wanted to get away from the barren land as quickly as possible. When they stopped for the night, a double guard was posted. Ramose didn't sleep well. The unfamiliar silence kept him awake. He suspected he wasn't the only one having trouble sleeping. Whenever he woke, there were always others shifting and stirring.

Once they were through this eerie stretch of country, they would reach the island of Sai where another fortress, originally built centuries ago by one of the old pharaohs, had been rebuilt and strengthened. That was where Hapu and his fellow soldiers would be garrisoned, ready to attack the rebels and bring them to heel.

The river was now so wide Ramose could barely see either shore. On the eastern side of the river, the rocky landscape was finally changing. On the western side, they saw the first village they'd seen for several days. It was stranded on a low hill surrounded by floodwater. The houses weren't built of mud bricks like the houses in Egypt. They were made of twigs and straw covering a framework of branches. The raging river waters had easily broken the fragile walls of the houses. More than a third of the village had been destroyed. Oxen and goats crowded on another small island, the water lapping at their feet. Ramose had seen the bloated bodies of drowned cattle further downstream. He wondered what the fate of these animals would be.

Even though the oarsmen were sweating and straining at the oars and the sail was full, the boat seemed to be moving in slow motion against the fast and furious current. Ramose had plenty of time to observe the worried faces of the villagers watching helplessly as the Nile ate away at their homes.

"The inundation is bigger this year," said Ramose. He had heard of times when the annual flooding of the Nile was greater than usual, when villages were destroyed by the fast-flowing waters. Cattle died, and people too. Ra's blessing could easily turn into Ra's curse.

The rowers were coming to the end of their two-hour shift at the oars. They were exhausted, their arms shaking from the pain in their muscles.

"Keep going," shouted the commander from his comfortable post at the stern of the boat. "You're

soldiers of Pharaoh's army. You'll have to with-
stand more than this."

The river suddenly narrowed as it squeezed
between the steep walls of a gorge. The water was
rushing through it at a frantic rate, crashing
against the rock cliffs, foaming and roaring
towards them. The oarsmen laboured and grunted with each stroke.

Ramose stood up to get a better view. "The oarsmen are worn out. We need a fresh crew before we
attempt to go through the gorge," he shouted at
the commander over the roar of the river. "Even
then, it's still dangerous."

The commander glared at Ramose. "Row
faster!" he shouted.

The boat entered the gorge. The rowers
strained and groaned. The boat's progress against
the current slowed even more. The oarsmen were
dipping their oars into the water as fast as they
could, at two or three times the pace that they
normally rowed. The raging water crashed into
the prow and broke over the sides soaking everyone. The boat was hardly moving forward at all.

Ramose called out to the commander again.
"We have to let the current take us back out of
the gorge. They'll never make it through this tor-
rent."

"I'm in charge," the commander shouted back.
"I'll make the decisions."

The commander yelled at the off-duty crew to take to the oars. Hapu glanced anxiously at Ramose, then hurried forward. It was no easy task to change over the crew in such conditions. The new crew had to take over the oars without missing a stroke. The boat was dipping and rocking, the deck was wet from the waves that were breaking over the prow. One man slipped as he stood to allow his replacement to take his place. His oar was ripped from his hand by the force of the water. Two other men stopped rowing, instinctively reaching out to catch the oar. The commander shouted orders at them, but no one could understand what he was saying over the roar of the water. The lost oar smacked against the rock wall and broke in two. With one oar gone and two momentarily stationary, the boat was carried by the current back the way it had come. It skewed to one side and hit a submerged rock. Then the stern crashed into the cliff face. The impact threw the commander and two soldiers into the water. The boat heeled to one side. Ramose tried to find something to hold on to as the sacks of wheat soaked up water and became heavy as rocks. He grabbed hold of the sternpost carved in the shape of a snake's head.

Hapu was yelling at his fellow soldiers. "Over to the other side! Keep your weight over on the other side."

The rest of the soldiers threw themselves to the other side of the boat trying to right it, but the force of the rushing water under its keel was too strong. The boat turned over like a child's toy and the soldiers were plunged into the raging waters. Ramose closed his eyes and clung onto the stern-post. He felt the cold water engulf him. He opened his eyes. The snake's head had been broken off and he was hanging on to the stern of an upturned boat. He let go.

The rushing waters carried him back down the gorge, tumbling him over and over as if he were no heavier than a papyrus stalk. His head bashed against the wall of the gorge. His arms and legs smashed against submerged rocks, but couldn't get hold of them. He tried to raise his arms to swim to the surface, but the force of the water made it impossible. He swallowed so much water he couldn't breathe. Something loomed towards him in the murky green water. It was a stone sculpture which must have fallen from another upturned boat. Ramose tried to move his heavy arms to turn his body away. He couldn't. The water was carrying him straight towards it.

Time seemed to slow. Ramose had time to realise that the statue was a hawk-headed figure of Ra. It was probably the last thing he'd ever see. He waited for the impact. Instead he felt large hands take hold of him. Perhaps it wasn't a statue after all. Perhaps it was the god himself waiting to take him on his journey through the underworld. "In the hands of Ra," Ramose thought.

Ramose could hear someone calling his name. Someone a long way away. "Ra is calling me," he thought. "He wants me to go with him."

"Ramose," said the voice of Ra.

Ramose felt a sharp pain on his cheek. He thought that Ra would have more magical means of getting his attention than slapping his face. He opened his eyes. A shape leaned over him. It was dripping on him. It wasn't Ra though. It was Hapu.

"Praise Amun, you're still alive," whispered Hapu and immediately disappeared from view.

Ramose got up on one elbow. The bright sunlight made it difficult for him to focus, or maybe it was the blood flowing from a cut above his eye. He felt warm squelchy mud beneath him. The sound of the rushing river was deafening. He looked around. Hapu was on his knees next to one of his fellow soldiers who was lying in the mud on the edge of the river. Ramose sat up. There were other soldiers cast on the mud bank. Some were face down. Some had their arms and legs bent at strange angles. One had a mask of raw flesh instead of a face. Hapu came back to him.

"Can you get up?" he asked in a shaky voice that didn't sound anything like Hapu.

"I think so," said Ramose as he moved his legs cautiously. "I don't think I've broken anything. You tend to the soldiers."

Hapu shook his head. "There's nothing I can do. They're all dead."

Hapu's face was lit by the light of the fire he had made. It was unmarked. Ramose had seen his own face reflected in a pool of water. It was cut and bruised like the rest of his body.

Hapu had still been on the boat when it over-turned. He had somehow managed to hold on to the upturned boat as it was flung around in the raging waters. A pocket of air had allowed him to breathe and he had been safe until the boat was finally smashed to pieces. Even then he had held on to a plank of wood.

By some miracle he had seen Ramose struggling beneath the surface and grabbed hold of him just before he was about to smash into the statue at the bottom of the river. Then he had let the river carry them where it wanted until an eddy took them to shore. The same current had deposited the bodies of other soldiers on the muddy bank.

"I've looked up and down the river bank," Hapu said. "I haven't found any other survivors."

"The rest may have been washed up further down river," said Ramose. "Some may have survived."

Hapu nodded, but Ramose knew he didn't believe that. The two boys stared into the fire. They had no food to cook. It didn't matter. Neither of them were hungry.

"Where do you think we are, Hapu?"

"I don't know. In the barren land somewhere."

"Do you think we're closer to Semna or to Sai?"

"I don't know, Ramose. It's hard to tell how long we were carried downstream. It seemed like hours, but it might have only been a few minutes."

A monkey screeched in the darkness. Then another. Soon there was a chorus of squawking. The animal noises set Ramose's nerves on edge. It sounded like the monsters of the underworld were calling to them. Just as suddenly the noise stopped. The silence was worse. Ramose had been in many foreign places, but he had never felt so threatened and defenceless.

"We'll make a decision in the morning," he said. His body ached all over, he was exhausted but he knew he wouldn't be able to sleep.

The monkeys started screeching again. There was the sound of a rock falling.

"Ramose!" shouted Hapu, staring back behind his friend. Ramose whipped round and saw dark figures appear out of the darkness. At first he thought they were huge monkeys come to attack them. Then he realised they were men, dark-skinned men. They were rebels. Two of them rushed towards him, pushed him to the ground and tied his hands behind him.

He tried to call out, though he knew there was no one for thousands of cubits who might come to their aid. One of the dark figures shoved something foul-tasting in his mouth to stop him from shouting. He tried to look around at Hapu. His friend was bound and gagged, just like him.

The rebels didn't speak. Not even to each other. They led them through the moonless darkness. There seemed to be nothing to mark the way. Each rock that Ramose stumbled over seemed the same as the last, but the rebels walked with confidence. They knew exactly where they were going. Ramose felt the ground beneath his feet rise steadily. After a while, a blank black shape loomed in front of them until it blotted out half the stars. The men pushed them through a ruined mud brick gateway.

Ramose blinked as the glare from a large fire blinded him. The flames threw shadows over huge walls that surrounded them on all sides. There were about twenty rebels around the fire. They weren't sitting though, they were all on their feet moving rhythmically around the flames to the beat of a drum. The dust rose in clouds as they stamped and whirled. From time to time, they let out strange whooping cries. Their faces were lost in concentration, deep in their own world. They spread their arms and turned all at the same time.

One of the rebels took the foul-tasting thing from Ramose's mouth. In the firelight, he could see that it was a screwed up strip of uncured animal skin. The rebel removed Hapu's gag as well.

"What are those men doing?" Hapu asked in a whisper.

"They're dancing," replied Ramose.

"It's the strangest sight I've ever seen," said Hapu. "I'd heard stories about barbarian men dancing, but I'd never imagined it like this."

Ramose remembered his own amazement when he'd first seen such dancing. In Egypt, men never danced, only women. There was a saying "stop dancing around like a barbarian" when a man was dithering and timid like a girl. The barbarian dance was nothing like the gentle floating movements of Egyptian dancing girls though. It was menacing. They didn't shake rattles and tambourines as they twirled. They waved sharpened sticks and axes.

As Ramose was pushed closer to the fire, he saw the faces of his captors for the first time. He realised that they were all boys, not much older than himself. They led him towards the only figure that wasn't dancing. He was sitting in what must have once been the chair of an Egyptian official. One armrest was broken and there were holes where jewels had been dug out. The boy was sitting in a confident pose with one foot resting on the opposite knee. When he saw Ramose, he sat up.

"This is an interesting catch that you've pulled out of the river," he said, leaning forward in his chair to peer at Ramose.

Ramose looked at the face that was examining him so closely. It was familiar. Ramose was dead tired and still stunned from his ordeal in the river. It took him a while to work out where he knew the face from.

"He's a bit battered, but if I'm not mistaken, what we have here is Prince Ramose, the pharaoh's brother."

The drumbeat stopped. The dancers stood still and turned to stare at the newcomers. Ramose glared at his captor.

"Kashta," he said. "Nice to see you again."

THE SONS
OF KUSH

HAPU turned to Ramose in surprise. "Perhaps you'd like to introduce me to your companion, Your Highness," Kashta said sarcastically.

"This is Hapu."

"A soldier?"

"Yes."

"We don't like Egyptian soldiers," said Kashta.

He got up to inspect Hapu. "They kill our people."

"He's a new recruit," replied Ramose. "He hasn't killed anyone."

Kashta walked around Hapu as if he was examining a donkey or an ox.

"Then we've got him just in time."

Ramose shook off the guards who were holding him and walked up to Kashta. "Where's Karoya?"

"I have no idea," replied Kashta. "It's not my fault if you can't keep track of your slaves."

"She isn't my slave. She never was. She disappeared the day you escaped. Where is she?"

"She's not here," said Kashta.

"When did you see her last?"

"You're the prisoner. I'm the one who asks the questions."

Kashta reached out a hand to touch Ramose's medallion.

"Very pretty," he said, pulling it over Ramose's head.

Ramose could hardly stand up, he was so exhausted. This last defiant act had drained him of what little energy he had left. As the barbarians took hold of him again, his knees crumpled and he collapsed into their grip.

"You'd better clean his wounds," said Kashta. "We have a hostage here. A royal Egyptian hostage. We don't want him dying. Not yet anyway."

Ramose and Hapu were led to a thatched hut and someone bathed Ramose's cuts and bruises. He could smell the sharp smell of the healing salve that Karoya had used on him before. It wasn't Karoya who was tending him though. It was a Kushite rebel, who was none too gentle and seemed to enjoy making Ramose cry out as he roughly rubbed the salve into his cuts. He felt a gourd cup pressed against his lips and he drank a bitter-tasting liquid. He had no idea what it was.

Ramose lay down on a mat woven from reeds. There was nothing else in the hut. Hapu was whispering something to him, but he couldn't quite hear.

Slats of sunlight penetrated the thin thatch of twigs above Ramose. The sun was hot. It took Ramose a moment to work out that he had been sleeping and, judging by the height and heat of the sun, sleeping for many hours. He looked around the flimsy hut. There was no sign of Hapu. His body ached all over. He felt like an old man as he struggled to get to his feet.

He tried to open the door but it was barred on the outside. The boy who was guarding the hut opened the door and let him out. Ramose blinked as he ducked through the low doorway and went out into the sunlight. Shading his eyes, he looked

around. The rebels had set up camp inside an old
fort. It was one of the string of forts built hundreds of years ago, but unlike the forts at Buhen
and Semna, this one hadn't been restored. The
mud brick walls still towered above, but their
tops were crumbling. Sand had blown into the
fort over the centuries and clumps of grass grew
here and there. What had once been neat rows of
barracks and administrative buildings was now
just a pile of broken mud bricks, half covered by
drifts of sand. An area had recently been cleared
and a few rough huts had been constructed.

"Ah, the prince has finally woken." Ramose
turned in the direction of a mocking voice.

The guard prodded him and Ramose went over
to where Kashta was sitting in his throne-like
chair as if he hadn't moved since the previous
day. The rebel was wearing Ramose's medallion.

"Where's Hapu?" Ramose demanded. He could
not see his friend anywhere.

"For a prisoner, you're very fond of asking questions," Kashta replied.

"I just want to know that he's safe."

"You seem to have a great interest in this
common soldier."

"He's a friend of mine. We've travelled far
together.'

"He's busy," said Kashta. "Where's the rest of
his company?"

"All drowned. Your men must have seen the bodies."

Kashta stood up and circled Ramose. There was no sign of the pleasant young man who had walked around the palace gardens with him. Ramose remembered how he had tricked him. The humiliation made his face burn. Now Kashta's mouth was set in a permanent sneer. He no longer wore an Egyptian kilt. Instead he wore a loincloth made from a piece of giraffe hide. His feet were bare and dusty. On the back of his head he wore a leather skullcap decorated with a number of ornaments carved from mother-of-pearl shell. The carvings were of animals: a crocodile, an ostrich, a strange creature with three heads.

A rebel brought a gourd containing a small helping of lumpy porridge and gave it to Ramose. Two other rebels were standing on either side of him. He tried to move into the shade, but they blocked his way. Ramose sat down on the dusty ground where he was and ate the food. They hadn't given him a spoon. He was hungry. He ate the porridge with his fingers.

"How does it feel to be a prisoner?" sneered Kashta. "It isn't very pleasant, is it?"

It wasn't the first time Ramose had been taken prisoner. He didn't need to be reminded what it was like. It wasn't pleasant at all.

Kashta had a stone flake in one hand and a reed pen and ink block in the other.

"Write a message to your brother, the pharaoh," he said, holding out the stone flake to Ramose. "Tell him you are held hostage by the Sons of Kush. If all Egyptian soldiers aren't withdrawn from Kush, you will be killed."

"It won't make any difference, Kashta," said Ramose, taking the writing materials. "I know you think I'm a useful hostage, but I'm not that important. The palace won't withdraw troops just because of me. They want Kush to be under Egyptian control. This rebellion will only make them more determined to subdue you."

"Will the pharaoh let his brother die?"

"Pharaoh is a ten-year-old boy," said Ramose. "He's not the one who makes decisions."

Kashta's sneer disappeared. "Who decides what Egypt will do? The vizier? The ministers?"

"The vizier is a good friend of mine and he would want to save me, but his first allegiance is to Egypt. The ministers don't like me at all. They would probably be pleased if I was out of the way. But it's not the ministers you have to worry about, they are just puppets."

"Who makes the decisions for Egypt?" asked Kashta.

"My sister," replied Ramose. "She is ruthless like my father. It's Princess Hatshepsut who tells the ministers what to do and she has no sisterly love for me. She would be delighted if you got me out of her way."

Kashta laughed. "I'm not a simple Kushite nomad," he said. "You can't fool me. Egypt is run by men, not a woman, a girl. Write the message."

"I need water," said Ramose, "to make the ink."

One of the rebels brought a gourd of water. Ramose chewed the end of the reed to make a brush and dipped it into the water. He sprinkled a few drops on the stone and muttered a prayer to Thoth, the god of writing. If ever he'd needed help from the gods, it was now.

Ramose rubbed the reed pen onto the ink block. He sat with the ink-laden brush poised. He hardly knew how to address his sister. He certainly didn't think anything he could say would stop her sending soldiers to attack Kushite rebels.

"Stop wasting time," said Kashta.

Ramose started to write.

Hatshepsut, your brother Ramose greets you.
I hope that you and our brother are well—may he have long life, health and prosperity. I have been captured by a band of rebels who call them-selves the Sons of Kush. You will perhaps be amused to hear that the leader of the group is Kashta, our recent guest in Thebes. He demands

that all Egyptian soldiers leave his country. If the oppression of Kush continues, he will kill me. I have told him that his demands will fall on deaf ears.

Ramose signed his name. The ink dried quickly in the heat. He handed the stone flake back to Kashta.

"It will take weeks for the message to get to Thebes and an answer to be sent back," said Ramose.

Kashta smiled. "Don't worry. I've got plenty of things to keep you busy."

Kasha sent Ramose to join Hapu, who was clearing sand. The rebel sat back in his chair and watched with pleasure.

The routine was the same for the next few days. Ramose and Hapu worked until midday and then they were imprisoned in the hut again. The thin thatch of twigs did a poor job of protecting them from the burning sun. The air in the hut was hot and stifling during the heat of the day. At night, it was cold and they had nothing but a putrid animal skin to keep them warm.

"We have to think of a way to escape," said Hapu as he ate his meagre lunch of stale bread and dried fish. "I'll starve otherwise."

Escape was the last thing on Ramose's mind. "I need to rest."

He handed Hapu his half-eaten meal and lay down. He immediately fell into a heavy sleep where he dreamed he was on a boat on the cool Nile, but the river wasn't in flood anymore. It was as calm as a pond. No, the river wasn't calm at all, the boat was being tossed back and forth by a strong wind.

"Ramose," the wind whispered. "Wake up."

Hapu was shaking him. "We have to try to escape."

Ramose was finding it hard to wake from his hot, heavy sleep.

"Look, I've cut through the door hinges. We can get out."

While Ramose had been sleeping, Hapu had been sawing away at the leather hinges of the door with a sharp stone.

"What about the guard?" said Ramose.

"He's asleep," whispered Hapu. "I can see him through the thatch."

Hapu gently lifted the door and pulled it aside. He peered out cautiously and then beckoned to Ramose as he edged out.

The rebels usually slept after they'd eaten their midday meal. Their guard, a boy no more than twelve years old, was curled up in the broken remains of a mud brick store opposite their hut. Ramose looked up on the wall. There was one lookout sitting dozing under a makeshift shade.

Hapu pointed towards a deep drift of sand that hadn't been cleared yet. They ducked behind it and made their way towards the gate on their hands and knees. The heat was unbearable. The noise of the cicadas seemed deafening. Ramose couldn't shake off his drowsiness. He didn't know what Hapu's plan was once they'd escaped from the fort, but he knew he needed to be more alert than he was now.

They got as close as they could to the gateway under cover of the sand and broken buildings. The cleared area stretched between them and the gate. Hapu looked around. The inner fort was deserted. Crouching low, he headed to the gate. Ramose followed him. They reached the gateway and then crept around the outside of the wall, flattening themselves against the crumbling mud bricks.

Ramose was beginning to think that they might really make their escape. His head finally started to clear as he imagined being on the river again just like in his dream. Then one of the young rebels emerged from behind a bush tying up his leopard skin loincloth. He was startled by the sight of the two Egyptian prisoners, pressed against the wall like lizards, but it only took him a moment to regain his composure. He pulled a dagger from his belt and called out to the guard. The dozing lookout jumped to his feet and raised the alarm. Hapu turned to run, but other rebels were already coming out of the gate. They were all armed with sticks and axes. Ramose looked at Hapu. The river would remain a memory.

As punishment for trying to escape, Kashta kept them confined in the stifling hut for two days. On the third day, the door was suddenly opened and Kashta stood in the doorway looking dark and dangerous with the bright light behind him.

"We're going on an expedition," he said. "I can't afford to leave anyone behind to guard you, so you'll have to come too."

Ramose sat up dazed and blinking. "Where are you going?"

"I'm not about to tell you my plans," said Kashta. "Here, you can carry my bows."

He handed three bows to Ramose. "Your friend can carry the water."

Unlike the other forts, this one had been built away from the Nile. It was perched on a range of inhospitable low hills. To the west, you could see the land that, hundreds of years before, had been cleared for farming by the original inhabitants of the fort. It was now barren and covered with drifts of sand. To the north and south, piles of bare rocks stretched into the distance. To the east, the hills gradually sloped down to the edge of the desert.

Kashta led the rebels and the two prisoners down from the broken gateway of the old fort. They were all armed, though Ramose noticed only a few of them had bows and daggers. The others carried roughly made stone axes and sharpened sticks.

"Don't try to escape," said Kashta. "My men have orders to kill you if you do."

Kashta's "men" chattered and joked. Like schoolboys, they pushed and jostled, trying to trip each other up. They headed down the steep path from the gateway and skirted around the lower slopes of the hills to the south.

The barren, rocky land was just as hostile as it had looked from the safety of the river. The rocks were sharp and cut through Ramose's flimsy reed sandals. The rebels walked barefoot and didn't seem concerned by the sharp stones which slid beneath their feet as they descended. The rebels laughed when Ramose slipped over.

They kept heading south as the sun got higher in the sky and the air grew hotter and hotter.

The rebels chattered noisily to each other or sometimes sang their strange rhythmic songs. They followed another path that slowly descended from the hills towards a grassy plain below. They were acting like they were on their way to a picnic, but Ramose decided they must be going hunting. After about two hours, Kashta held up his hand. The rebels stopped talking and moved forward more cautiously, ducking down so that the surrounding rocks concealed them. Ramose peered ahead, trying to see what they were looking at. Several hands pulled him down roughly.

"Get down, Prince," said Kashta. "We don't want our quarry to see us."

They crept forward and finally Ramose could see what their target was. Below them, in a rocky valley which had been hidden from view until now, was an Egyptian encampment. It was actually a Kushite gold mine, but Egyptian soldiers had taken it over.

Egypt had its own gold mines, but Egyptians had become so hungry for gold that there weren't enough mines to provide all the gold they needed. Kush was a wild and desolate place on the surface, but below its desert soils there was a wealth of gold. It was one of the main reasons the Egyptians had wanted to invade Kush.

Mining for gold was hard, backbreaking work. Ramose could see men chipping large blocks of stone from holes in the earth. It was a slow process using copper chisels. They dragged the blocks to the surface and then a fire was lit beneath the blocks so that they cracked and split and revealed the veins of gold. The gold-bearing rock was then crushed and carried away to be heated in a furnace to extract the molten gold.

The people doing the hard work were all Kushite slaves. A dozen Egyptian soldiers guarded them.

Kashta signalled to his men to prepare to attack. First the rebels painted their faces, turning the joking boys into frightening warriors. They tied up their prisoners' hands and feet so that they couldn't escape during the attack. The rope was roughly woven from grass, but it effectively immobilised them. They were also gagged so that they couldn't call out and warn the Egyptians. Then some of the rebels positioned themselves behind the rocks and loaded their bows. The rest held ready their axes and sharpened sticks.

Ramose looked down at the unsuspecting Egyptian soldiers below. Some were leaning on rocks talking to each other. Others were sitting in the shade carving arrowheads. He wished there was some way that he could warn them.

"I'm glad you're going to witness this, Prince," whispered Kashta. His face was striped with white and red. His eyes glinted with the anticipation of the battle. His mouth was pulled back in a wild grin.

Then, with a signal from Kashta, the rebels clambered over the rocks and down into the valley, yelling and screaming like demons. The Egyptian soldiers ran around in confusion, not knowing who or what was attacking them. The rebels shot arrows at those who tried to escape from the valley. Ramose watched in horror as two Egyptians fell to the ground.

The slaves were confused too. It took a while for the rebels to convince them that they were being freed. Many of them ran and hid. Some fell at the feet of their liberators, calling out praise to whatever gods they worshipped. Kashta yelled at them to join the rebels, fight their oppressors, but though a few joined in the fight, most of them stayed cowering behind rocks.

Ramose noticed one slave who wasn't afraid. She was a female slave with short-cropped hair. Before the attack, she had been making bread over a small fire. She must have been a troublesome slave as her ankles were tied together. She let the rebels cut the ropes, but didn't thank her liberators. She picked up a length of faded cloth and draped it over her head. Ignoring the chaos around her, she calmly found a leather water-bag and filled it from a jar. Ramose's heart thumped faster inside his chest. He hadn't recognised her at first. The short hair and the ragged kilt had fooled him. He was certain now. It was Karoya.

7

NIGHT AND DAY

R AMOSE felt a rush of joy. It hadn't been due to his own skill or cunning, but he had found Karoya. He tried to call out to her, but his mouth was full of the stinking animal hide. He tried to get Hapu's attention, but he was busily sawing away at his bonds on the sharp edge of a rock. He had to let Karoya know that he was there. He couldn't run after her because he was tied hand and foot like a hobbled donkey. She was walking away. Ignoring all the noise and conflict, she was making her own quiet escape.

Ramose tried to struggle to his feet, but couldn't. He crawled up over the rocks that were concealing him, hardly noticing the way they cut into his knees. Hapu looked up, puzzled by his friend's actions. Ramose tried to stand again but he lost his footing and tumbled down the steep slope, causing a cascade of smaller rocks.

Karoya looked back over her shoulder at the sound of the clattering rocks. Ramose slid head-first down the slope and came to a halt halfway down. He wriggled around so that he could see Karoya. She was scanning the rocks, trying to find the cause of the noise, in case it was a threat to her escape. He raised his bound hands trying to attract her attention. Just for a moment, her eyes met Ramose's. His mouth tried to smile, but the gag wouldn't let it. Ramose felt elated, despite his cuts and bruises, despite the fact that he was tied up and sprawled upside down on the side of a hill. He knew that she'd seen him. But then Karoya turned and quickly walked away. Without turning back, she scrambled over the rocks on the opposite side of the valley and disappeared from view.

The Egyptian soldiers had regrouped. Someone had taken command. They were fewer in number, but they were better armed and better trained than the rebels. The rebels' confidence faded and they ran around without listening to Kashta, who was yelling orders, trying to get them organised. Ramose was hardly aware of the continuing battle though. He stared at the opposite side of the valley, at the blank wall of rock where Karoya had disappeared. Why hadn't she come to help him? She hadn't even smiled when she'd seen him.

Ramose felt like he was in a dream. The shouts and yells from the battle below sounded distant and unreal. There was something strange about the light. The green of the few tufts of grass was deeper, the colour of the sandy earth richer, the way it was when the sun was getting low in the sky. Except that it wasn't even midday.

Hapu had managed to cut through the rope tying his hands. He quickly undid his feet and pulled the gag from his mouth. He scrambled down to Ramose and dragged him back to safety.

"Are you all right?" he asked as he untied Ramose's feet.

Ramose nodded, though in fact his neck was hurting from being twisted in the fall. He moved his head from side to side, back and forward. Then he noticed the sun.

"Look. Look at the sun," he said. "There's a piece missing."

Hapu looked up. Both boys stared in fear and confusion. It was as if someone had taken a sharp blade and cut a slice off the sun. A dark sliver had taken its place.

Ramose shielded his eyes. As he watched, the missing piece grew bigger.

"Something's eating it," said Hapu, his voice quavering. "It's Apophis. Apophis is defeating Ra."

"That can't be," said Ramose. "It's day. Ra's day-time journey across the heavens is never challenged. It's at night that he has to fight the serpent-god Apophis. And Ra always defeats him. Always."

"Apophis must have tricked Ra," said Hapu. "He's attacked him during the day. And he's beating him."

Ramose shook his head. He had a terrible feeling. Ra wasn't being defeated, surely that could never happen. Ra was angry. A quarter of the sun had now been replaced with blackness and the light was dimming. Others had noticed now. There were cries of surprise and fear echoing around the valley. From somewhere in the distance came the howling of a hyena. Rebels and Egyptians alike stopped fighting and fell to their knees bowing their heads to the earth in terrified prayer. The recently freed slaves panicked, their new-found bravery disappearing as they tried to find somewhere to hide from this awful event. There was nowhere to hide though. Only half the sun was left.

"Ra is deserting us," said Ramose, his voice trembling. "He's going to leave us in eternal darkness."

Ramose was certain now that Ra was angry—angry with Egypt, but especially angry with him. He had ignored his duty to Ra's land. He had wandered around the world outside Egypt, doing what he pleased. Only a slice of the sun remained. He should have noticed the signs before. First, there had been the defeat of Egypt's powerful armies on three fronts, even though Egypt had more men and better arms. Then the inundation had been too great, destroying villages and farmland, drowning soldiers, almost taking his own life. Now this. A terrible black disc surrounded by an eerie halo of yellow had taken the place of the sun. The birds suddenly stopped calling. The howling of the hyena trailed off. The Egyptians and rebels all fell silent. Ramose shivered. It was as dark as night.

"It's the end of the world," whispered Hapu.

He was right. Crops wouldn't grow without sunlight. The people of Egypt would stumble around in darkness for a while and then they would die of hunger.

Ramose closed his eyes and started to pray.

"Praise to thee, Ra," he murmured. "Most glorious of gods, who is beautiful at morning and evening. Lord of Eternity, Creator of Everlastingness, do not abandon us. Shine your beams of light upon our faces. Flood the world with your light."

Ramose fell to his knees and repeated the prayer over and over again. He promised offerings. He vowed that if the sun god returned to the sky, he would never think about his own desires again. He would do his duty and serve Pharaoh and Egypt as he should.

"Look," shouted Hapu. "Ra is returning to us."

Ramose opened his eyes and looked up at the dark sky. A splinter of light had appeared at the edge of the terrible black disc. His prayers were working.

As they watched, the slice of brightness grew. The darkness was fading. The birds started calling again. In a few minutes, the black part of the disc was smaller than the golden piece. Ra was not abandoning them. Others looked up and shouted praise to Ra as the last trace of black disappeared.

"Ra lives," shouted Hapu, tears running down his face. "The blazing one strides across the heavens again."

Egyptians, rebels and slaves cheered and shouted. Ramose felt a wave of relief as the sunlight warmed his skin. The rebels were the first to remember the conflict. They had been losing the battle. While the Egyptians were still on their knees in prayer, the rebels started to retreat. Ramose's happiness suddenly went cold. He turned to Hapu.

"I saw Karoya," he said, trying to pull the cords from his hands. "She was one of the slaves. We have to find her."

"You're not going anywhere," said Kashta who had come up behind them with the rest of the rebels and some of the freed slaves. Two of the rebels had been wounded and were being supported by their friends.

"But…" Ramose was about to tell Kashta he had seen Karoya, but changed his mind. He didn't understand why she had walked away from the mine, but at least she hadn't joined Kashta's band of rebels.

Kashta looked back at the valley. The Egyptians were getting up and looking around, realising that their attackers had slipped away. The rebel leader grabbed Ramose and pulled him along with him as he ran from the valley.

"Don't think you can get away, Prince." Kashta was trying to sound as confident as ever, but Ramose could tell that the appearance of the black disc in the sky had shaken him. The people of Kush worshipped the sun the same as

Egyptians, even though they had a different name for it.

The rebels retraced their steps, hurrying back towards the safety of their hidden camp.

"We can slow down now," Kashta said when he was sure that the Egyptians weren't following them. "Your countrymen are more interested in holding on to their gold than catching us."

The rebels talked in low voices to each other in their own language. No doubt they were trying to make sense of what had just happened. Once they were safely away from the mine, they began singing and chanting as they walked. It was hard to believe that this ragged group of boys had come close to defeating the Egyptian soldiers.

"I don't know what you're all so happy about," said Ramose as he walked beside Kashta. "You lost the battle."

"Perhaps, but we freed the slaves and many of them joined us," replied Kashta. "Only two rebels were wounded."

"It was hardly a victory, you had to run away. And you only got away safely because the sun disappeared."

"I have seen the strength of our enemy," replied Kashta. "I know what we're up against. The only way we can free Kush from the chains of Egypt is by many small victories like today's. The Sons of Kush will triumph eventually."

It sounded like a well-rehearsed speech that Kashta had delivered many times before. Nevertheless, Ramose was beginning to think that the rebels could eventually wear down the might of Egypt, like a dog worrying at the legs of a leopard.

Kashta called out to the other rebels. They leapt in the air cheering and ran ahead dragging Hapu with them.

"What did you say to them?" asked Ramose.

"I told them that we are going to do some hunting on the way back to the fort, so that we can celebrate our success with a feast."

The rebels left the narrow track in the bare hills and headed down to the plain. The flat land stretched out as far as they could see to the east. The plain was covered in dry, spiky grass. This dull expanse was occasionally broken by a spindly acacia tree, its branches almost bare of leaves, or a small clump of tangled tamarisks. Kashta and Ramose were the last to reach the plain. The other rebels were ahead. A pair of gazelle suddenly leapt up out of the swaying grass. The rebels set off after them with a whoop, pulling Hapu along with them.

"Tell me what happened to Karoya," Ramose asked.

Kashta shook his head. "I don't have to tell you anything, Prince."

He stopped to break a branch from an acacia.

"I just want to know what she's doing," said Ramose, "that she's safe."

"She has chosen her own road to follow," Kashta replied, using the branch to beat a path through the long grass.

Ramose didn't like the grassland. The grass was up to their knees. Ramose preferred to be able to see where he was putting his feet. Kashta laughed at the timid way Ramose stepped through the long grass.

"There could be snakes hiding in the grass," he said, parting the grass cautiously. "Or leopards or hyenas."

Kashta laughed again, beating the grass aside as if it hid nothing more dangerous than field mice.

"You expect Karoya to be loyal to you, but she won't," said Kashta. "No matter how friendly you were to her, she was still Egypt's slave."

"But she had an important position in Sai," replied Ramose.

"She had to make sure that her own people obeyed the laws of an oppressor. It wasn't something she enjoyed doing."

"How do you know?" asked Ramose hotly, resenting the rebel's knowledge of his friend.

"She told me. Her first loyalty will always be to Kush."

"I don't believe you. She said she liked her job."

"Why would she tell you what is in her heart?"

Ramose remembered the cold look he had seen in Karoya's eyes not long before. He was starting to wonder if he had ever known her true feelings.

The rebels guarding Hapu were out of sight in front of them. Kashta absently hit out with his stick at the grass stalks, which were now almost up to their waists. Something whipped up out of the grass, so quick it was impossible to see what it was until it stopped just as suddenly.

It was a cobra as thick as the top of Ramose's arm and striped with broad bands of yellow and black. It reared up, its spotted hood opening out on either side of its head, its yellow eyes level with Kashta's face, staring right at him. Kashta stood frozen. The snake's tongue flickered. Its venom-filled teeth glistened. Kashta still didn't move. Ramose didn't know a lot about snakes, but he knew that this one was angry and ready to strike. He remembered snake charmers who had been brought to the palace as entertainment.

"Move your stick from side to side," he whispered.

Kashta didn't respond. He was staring into the snake's terrible eyes, mesmerised.

"Do as I say, Kashta."

Kashta held up his stick with shaking hands and moved it slowly from side to side. The movement attracted the snake's attention. The hooded head of the snake swayed with the motion of the stick. In one swift motion Ramose pulled Kashta's knife from his belt, took a firm grip and swung the blade in an arc. The blade dug into the snake at the back of its head. The force of his blow knocked the snake to the ground. The knife went right through the snake and pinned it to the earth. The snake writhed and twisted. It was at least six cubits long. Ramose felt its scaly tail whip the back of his hand. Its strength surprised him. He almost thought it would pull the knife from the earth, but it was the snake's death spasms. The writhing slowed until the snake lay dead.

Kashta was still stunned. His eyes were wide. They had just stared death in the face. All traces of his bravado disappeared. Ramose pulled out the knife. The snake lay lifeless. Ramose got to his feet, the knife still in his hand. Kashta made no attempt to wrest the weapon from him. Ramose wiped the knife on the grass and held it out grip first to Kashta.

"Come on," he said. "We'd better catch up with the others."

Kashta moved at last. Slowly, he took the knife from Ramose. Ramose picked up the dead snake. The two boys walked slowly back towards the hills.

"You could have escaped," Kashta said.

"I'd just get lost if I wandered off into this strange land," he said. "And anyway, I wouldn't go without Hapu. There'll be another time to escape. When my sister doesn't respond to the letter you sent, you'll get sick of feeding us."

The two boys climbed the rocky slopes. After a while they could see the other rebels ahead of them. They were carrying a dead gazelle, singing and chanting noisily.

When they caught up, the rebels chattered excitedly. Ramose couldn't understand what they were saying, but he got the idea that they thought their catch was a lot more impressive than their leader's. Kashta looked at the snake and shrugged. He didn't explain how the snake had come to be killed.

That evening the rebels celebrated long into the night. They roasted the gazelle on a spit and Kashta allowed them to take some beer, stolen from Egyptians, from their store. The rebels danced and chanted as if they had defeated the entire Egyptian army.

Ramose watched the boys dancing after Hapu had gone to bed. Their faces were deep in concentration as they stamped and twirled, raising clouds of dust. Kashta was skinning the snake.

"You think the dancing is strange, don't you?" Kashta asked.

"In Egypt, dancing is something that only women do. Men would never dream of dancing."

"Do your women dance like this?" he asked, indicating the stomping rebels.

"No," said Ramose, smiling at the thought of the delicate palace dancers thumping around the western hall. "They dance lightly and slowly. It's an entertainment."

Kashta jumped up. "Come and dance with us," he said as he joined the dancers.

Ramose shook his head.

"Come on, Prince," said Kashta. "No one will see you but us."

Ramose got to his feet and walked over to the fire. Kashta pulled him into the circle of dancers. Ramose clumsily tried to copy the rebels' movements.

"Move your feet, Ramose," Kashta said as he whirled around. "Feel the music. Tonight we are dancing to celebrate success. At other times it can help release pain and frustration."

Ramose started to move with the circle of rebels. Slowly at first he moved with the rhythm of the drums. He stamped his feet in the dust. He felt his anger at being held prisoner and he danced faster. He remembered Karoya's blank face as she'd looked at him. He stamped harder. He twisted and turned around the fire. Then he remembered how he'd killed the snake.

He remembered his realisation, his duty to Egypt and his brother. He spread out his arms, closed his eyes and turned, letting the sound of the rebels' chanting fill his head. He wouldn't give up. He'd have to wait for his chance, get away from the rebels and return to Egypt. He twirled faster and faster. He could do it. He opened his eyes and the fort was spinning around him. He fell into the dust. The rebels laughed. Ramose laughed too.

Kashta helped Ramose to his feet. The two boys moved away from the dancers and sat down panting, their bodies wet with sweat despite the cold night air. They watched the dancers in silence until their breathing slowed. Kashta took the medallion from around his neck and handed it to Ramose.

"You saved my life today," Kashta said.

"I was as concerned about my life as yours," replied Ramose, fingering the cobra design on his medallion.

"Why didn't you let the snake kill me? I'm your enemy."

Ramose shrugged. "I don't think of people in terms of allies and enemies. I've made mistakes doing that before. Some of my best friends were originally people who I was sure were my enemies." Ramose stared into the fire. He had a sudden vision of his sister when she was younger and they still played together. "The dearest person to me turned out to be the one who wished me most ill." The image of the smiling young girl was replaced by the woman with the cold eyes who never smiled.

The dancers finally stopped and drifted off to their huts to sleep. The flames died down.

"Karoya escaped from me at Semna," said Kashta suddenly. "I'd spent weeks trying to win her over to our cause, but she refused. I tied her up every night to stop her escaping, but she somehow managed to cut herself free."

"I saw her today," said Ramose. "She was one of the slaves at the mine."

Kashta turned to Ramose, surprised.

"I didn't see her," he said.

"Her hair was cut short. I didn't recognise her at first. She escaped during the fight."

"She told me she didn't want to take sides," said Kashta. "All she wanted was to return to the desert."

"She saw me," said Ramose.

"Are you sure?"

"I'm sure," replied Ramose sadly. "She looked right into my eyes and then she turned and walked away."

Kashta put his hand on Ramose's shoulder. "She has her own life to live."

Ramose got to his feet. "I'm exhausted."

Kashta nodded. "It's been a long day."

Ramose went back to the hut where Hapu was snoring loudly. There was no one guarding the hut, but he was too tired to think about escaping. He lay down wearily, pulling the smelly animal skin around him. It wasn't enough to keep him warm. Hapu turned in his sleep.

"I thought you were going to stay up all night," he said sleepily.

"I've been talking to Kashta," said Ramose.

Hapu opened one eye. "You shouldn't be so friendly with the enemy," he complained. "It's not good military strategy."

Ramose laughed. "We'll see. Sooner or later he'll realise that I'm not a useful hostage and then I hope instead of slitting our throats he'll just let us go."

Part of him was feeling sad that Karoya had appeared so briefly only to disappear, probably forever. But there was also a part of him that was pleased, pleased that he'd made some headway with Kashta. He felt that it was only a matter of time until the rebel let them go.

8

THE VOICE OF RA

Ramose was woken by bright sunlight in his face. He felt like he hadn't been asleep for long, yet the sun was burning his skin. He opened his eyes. The light was glaring. Usually there were just thin bars of light between the sticks and twigs that made up the hut. Ramose suddenly realised why there was more sunlight than usual. The door of the hut was wide open.

Hapu was still snoring softly. Ramose got up and went to the door. There was no guard. He went out into the full sun. The sun was just over the fort wall. Half of the cleared area was in sunlight, the other half was still in shade. No one else was awake. Ramose looked up at the battlements. There was no lookout. The only two rebels in sight were both asleep: one face down in a pile of straw, the other curled up like a cat on a length of animal skin. They were both in the shaded half of the fort. Ramose didn't have long. The line where the shadow met the sunlight was creeping towards the rebel sleeping on the animal skin.

He ducked back into the hut and shook Hapu.

"Is it my shift at the oars?" he asked sleepily.

Ramose put his hand over his friend's mouth.

"Wake up, Hapu," he whispered. "The door of the hut is open. The rebels are still sleeping. We can escape."

Hapu blinked a few times and then got to his feet. The two boys crept out of the hut.

"We'll need water," whispered Hapu.

Ramose stopped. He looked at the water jars which were in the shaded half of the fort over near Kashta's hut. He looked at the gate. The huge wooden doors had fallen from their hinges many years before. They leaned at angles up against the crumbling gateway. The world outside was visible between them. The advancing sunlight was less than a cubit from the rebel curled up on the animal skin. As soon as the hot sunlight reached him, he would wake. It was only a day's march to the river. They had walked much further without water before. Ramose turned to Hapu and shook his head. It was too risky.

They crept towards the gateway, glancing anxiously over their shoulders at every second step. The gateway towered over them. Ramose couldn't believe their luck. Was Ra on his side at last? Had the great god forgiven him? There was still no sign of movement within the fort. Hapu turned to Ramose. The two boys grinned at each other. They walked faster, passing under the gateway. They started to run. Ramose glanced back one last time. He turned away from the fort and ran straight into something. Someone. It was a man, a huge man with black skin wearing nothing but a leopard skin loincloth. He wasn't the only one. Another had a hold of Hapu.

Rough unfriendly hands bound Ramose's wrists and ankles tightly with strips of animal hide. He was dragged back inside the fort between two men and forced to his knees in front of a third. Hapu was pushed down beside him. The sound of shouting voices had woken Kashta and his rebels. They drifted sleepily from their huts. When they saw the newcomers, they looked as frightened as Ramose and Hapu.

Six men stood in front of them. They were Kushites the same as Kashta, but older and meaner looking. They stared down at Hapu and Ramose with grim faces. Kashta came over to the men with his head hanging. One man was obviously the leader. He ripped Ramose's medallion from around his neck and started shouting at Kashta. Ramose couldn't understand a word of what he was saying. Kashta replied meekly. He tried to say something in reply, but the man cut him off angrily.

Kashta turned to Ramose. "Psaro says that he will give the pharaoh another two weeks to reply to my demands. After that he will cut off one of your fingers for every week that Egyptian soldiers remain in Kush."

Ramose looked up in horror at Kashta.

"The message would have barely reached Thebes," he protested. "It would take another four weeks at least to get a reply and anyway, I've told you, my sister doesn't care about me."

"I've told my father this," said Kashta miserably. "He won't listen."

Ramose had guessed that Psaro and his men were the real rebels. He hadn't realised that this rebel leader was also Kashta's father.

Hapu sat in the prison hut with his arms folded across his chest, his fingers hidden in his armpits.

"He's bluffing isn't he?" he said. "He wouldn't really cut off our fingers."

"It's my fingers he's planning to cut off, not yours," replied Ramose. "And I don't think he's bluffing at all. He means it."

Hapu peeped out between the twigs that made up the door to their prison. Outside there was a burly guard with a dagger and an axe hanging from his belt. Up on the battlements two lookouts were patrolling with bows.

"We should have made more of an effort to escape before."

Ramose wiggled his fingers nervously. Escaping from Kashta's young rebels suddenly seemed ridiculously easy. Escaping from the real rebels seemed impossible.

The days passed slowly. Ramose and Hapu were kept locked in the stifling hut all day. At nightfall, they were allowed out for a few minutes, given a meagre meal and then locked up again. They were always hungry and the hut stank of urine.

During the days they could hear sounds of activity. More rebels arrived. Each evening they emerged from their prison to find the darkened fort more and more in order. Kashta's boys had only cleared a small space among the sand drifts inside the fort and built a few ramshackle huts.

The rebels had now cleared all the area and were rebuilding the collapsed mud brick barracks. Every evening the piles of stores were bigger than they had been the evening before, more of the gateway had been repaired and a team of weary men returned from outside the fort. Ramose guessed that they were digging a surrounding trench. This wasn't just a temporary camp for the rebels: it was going to be their headquarters.

Ramose hungrily ate the bread and meat that they had been given for their evening meal. He'd eaten worse food on his travels, but there just wasn't enough to satisfy his hunger.

"It's been thirteen days since Psaro and his men arrived," said Ramose.

Hapu nodded miserably. Ramose inspected his fingers in the fast dimming light. He had no doubts that Psaro's threat was serious. He had tried hard to think of a way that they could escape. Every day he'd racked his brain, but it was impossible. There were too many rebels and, unlike Kashta's boys, they were well disciplined.

Ramose woke from a terrible dream about a dagger dripping blood. In the dream, he'd been too frightened to look down to see if a finger was missing. He opened his eyes. He could just make out his fingers in the light from the rebels' fire. As far as he could tell, they were all there. Psaro was talking to his men. Ramose had no idea what he was saying, but from the tone, it sounded like he was explaining some sort of plan or strategy.

Suddenly Ramose heard another voice. A louder voice. It sounded like it was coming down from the sky. It had a strange unearthly sound to it. He thought that he must be still asleep. The voice spoke again. Ramose couldn't understand what it was saying. He sat up and shook Hapu awake.

"Something's happening," he said.

As Hapu stirred sleepily, Ramose looked through the cracks in the wall of the hut. There was a bright light shining down into the fort courtyard. Shadows played back and forth like ghosts. The voice spoke again, even more loudly. There was a frightened murmur outside the hut. The rebels were all looking up at the light, shielding their eyes from its brilliance.

A bright white figure was hovering above the wall of the fort. It had a hawk head and long white robes which whipped and flapped in the growing breeze.

"It's Ra," whispered Ramose. It was weeks since the sun had disappeared and Ramose had promised to do his duty and serve Egypt. He hadn't kept his promise. He hadn't even managed to escape from the rebels.

Hapu peered through the branches that made up the hut wall. "You were right, Ramose," he said in a frightened voice. "Ra is angry with us. Now he's come to kill us."

Ramose broke away some twigs trying to get a better view. He could see the sharp beak of the hawk head in the light. The blank eyes looked down, scanning the rebels huddled below as if searching for someone. Ramose thought he knew who the sun god was looking for. Ra raised his arms. White robes flapped from them like giant wings. The voice boomed out again. Karoya had taught Ramose a few words of Kushite, but he couldn't make out any of what the god had said.

Whatever it was, it had an effect on the rebels. They all fell to their knees and bowed their heads to the ground.

"He's speaking in the language of Kush," Ramose said. "He must be telling the rebels to bring us to him."

There was a noise outside the hut. The door suddenly flew open. Kashta was standing outside.

"Come with me," he said. He had a sheet of bark in his hand, rolled in the shape of a cone.

"No!" cried Hapu. "We won't. We're not ready to die."

"I'm helping you escape," he said. "Quick. We don't have a lot of time."

Hapu and Ramose didn't move.

"You saved my life. Now I am saving yours," the rebel said to Ramose. "You have to trust me."

"Don't listen to him." said Hapu. "It's a trick."

Ramose had no idea what the rebel was doing, but he jumped to his feet and followed Kashta. Hapu hesitated, but then followed his friend. Kashta ran to a set of newly repaired steps that led up to the battlements. The rebels were all on their knees, even Psaro, muttering prayers to Ra.

"Up here," he said breathlessly. "You'll find a rope at the top where you'll be able to let yourself down over the wall."

"Then where will we go?" asked Hapu.

"Ra will guide you," said Kashta, his face flashing with a sudden smile. He grasped Ramose's arm. "Good luck."

Ra hadn't spoken since Kashta had come to the prison hut. The rebels, unused to saying prayers, were running out of things to say to the god. Ramose and Hapu ran up the steps. Just as Kashta had said, there was a rope secured to one of the battlements. It disappeared over the side of the wall. Hapu pulled it, testing its weight. He let himself down over the side. Ramose glanced down into the fort. Psaro was looking up at them. He struggled to his feet with an angry roar.

Ramose grabbed hold of the rope and followed Hapu. As he lowered himself over the edge, he looked over at the figure of Ra, its arms still outstretched. He could see that the light was coming from two flaming torches. Ra turned towards him. The white-robed figure dropped its arms and moved towards him along the top of the wall, drifting towards him in its flapping white robes. Ramose scrambled to lower himself over the side, burning his hands in his hurry to get down. He looked up. The white figure of the god was climbing down the rope after him. Ramose lost his grip and fell the rest of the way, almost ten cubits, landing on top of Hapu. The two boys collapsed in a heap. They struggled to their feet, just as the god landed lightly beside them.

"That was a very undignified exit," said the god, in a familiar voice.

It lifted off its hawk head, revealing the smiling face of Karoya beneath it. Ramose and Hapu stood staring in amazement. The sounds of angry voices coming from the gateway told them that the rebels knew they had been duped.

Ramose and Hapu both started to ask questions at once.

"We must go," said Karoya, throwing off the long robes. "Quick. This way."

9

BETWEEN WORLDS

KAROYA disappeared into the night. Ramose and Hapu hurried after her. Ramose had no idea where she was leading them. He didn't really care as long as it was away from the rebels. Ramose soon lost his sense of direction. He assumed Karoya would be heading for the river, but several hours later, when the first light started to lighten the eastern horizon, Ramose could see no sign of the river. The sky turned pink and Karoya still kept going.

When the sun had risen and the sky was bright, she finally came to a stop. Ramose looked up at the sun. It had been two weeks since he'd seen the sun's disc unbarred by the branches of his prison.

"We can't stay out in the daylight," Karoya said.

She clambered over a rocky outcrop and then disappeared. Ramose and Hapu followed her into a small cave.

Inside the cave, a single oil lamp was burning. When their eyes got used to the dim light, the boys could see that Karoya had been living in the cave for some time. There was a store of food and the glowing remains of a small fire. She rekindled the fire and prepared some food.

"I thought you really were a god come to Earth," said Hapu, burning his tongue on the hot bread that Karoya handed to him.

"Where did you get the hawk mask and the robes?" Ramose blew on his bread to cool it.

"Sometime ago, the rebels ambushed a boat that was taking supplies to a temple at Tombos They took the food, but they had no use for the priest's robes."

"And how did you make your voice sound so deep and loud?" asked Hapu. "That's what convinced me it really was Ra."

Karoya smiled. "That wasn't my voice. It was Kashta's. He made himself sound louder by speaking through a cone of bark."

Ramose nodded. "Very clever."

"How did you know where we were?"

"News travels fast among the people of Kush."

"We didn't see any people, apart from Kashta's rebels."

"Kushites prefer to keep away from Egyptians. We are very good at blending into the landscape."

"And how did you get Kashta to help?"

"I came into the camp with some serving women. I spoke to Kashta then. Kashta never wanted you to come to harm. He agreed to help me free you."

After the food, Hapu soon fell asleep in the dry grass that Karoya had collected for them to sleep on. Ramose knew he should have felt tired, he'd been walking all night. His legs ached from the unaccustomed exertion, but he was wide awake.

"I thought you were walking away forever when I saw you at the gold mine."

"I didn't have time to explain."

"I knew you'd seen me, but it was like you were looking right through me."

"I wasn't sure what I was going to do then."

Ramose looked up at Karoya.

"You mean you were considering walking away forever?"

"I had been captured as a slave to labour in a mine, probably till I died of exhaustion. I wanted to get as far away from Egyptians as possible."

"Including me."

"I knew you'd be able to get away from Kashta eventually."

"What changed your mind?"

"I was about to head into the desert, when I overheard some men who were going to join Psaro's rebels. They said they were going to the fort where Psaro's son was holding an Egyptian prince captive."

She put out her tiny fire with a handful of sand.

"I was sure Kashta would not harm you, but I had heard stories of Psaro's cruelty."

Ramose glanced down at his hands resting on his knees. He wiggled his fingers.

"You've saved me again, Karoya."

Karoya smiled. "It seems every time I turn my back, you get yourself into some trouble or other."

Ramose lay down in the soft, sweet-smelling grass. When he awoke he'd have to decide what to do next. He'd have to head out into the dangerous world again. For the moment, he could enjoy the feeling of safety and comfort for the first time in weeks. He had everything he needed in the cool cave. He was asleep in moments.

No one was in a hurry to leave the security of the cave the following day. It was the first time the three friends had been together for a long time. While Karoya's store of food held out, they were all content to rest in the coolness and talk about old times. In the evening, Ramose ventured out to look at the stars. For the moment, he didn't miss the sun.

It was Hapu who was the first to face his responsibilities. "I have to get back to the river," he said.

"Where will you go?" asked Ramose.

"I'll continue on to Sai," he replied. "I'll join another battalion there."

"Do you still want to fight the rebels?" asked Ramose.

"I'm a soldier in Pharaoh's army. I'm not free to wander around as I please. If I am commanded to fight them, I will." Hapu looked at his friend. "What about you, Ramose?"

"Now that I know Karoya is safe, I'll go back to Thebes," he said. "I have to be there to advise my brother."

Ramose's purpose had been clear to him since the day of Ra's disappearance. Ra was angry with him because he wasn't doing his duty as a royal son of Egypt. His job was simple. It was to protect the young pharaoh, to support him through the difficult time when he was too young to rule alone. He had to make sure that Hatshepsut didn't quash the boy's spirit and take control.

"I'm the same as you, Hapu," he said. "I can't just wander around wherever I want. I also have my duty to Egypt."

"And you, Karoya?" asked Hapu.

Karoya didn't reply straight away. She sat shaping dough into flat discs as she had done on many other occasions when the three had travelled together.

"I don't know what to do," she said. "I want my people to be free from Egypt's oppression, but I don't want to be at war with Egypt."

She placed the circles of dough on hot stones to bake them.

"I have lost my place in the world," she said quietly.

Ramose knew exactly how his friend felt. They had a lot in common. They had both lost their closest family members. At a young age, they had been thrown from the only life they had known into a different world. Their lives had changed forever. Now they found that they belonged in neither world.

"What can I do to help you?"

"There is nothing you can do, Ramose," Karoya finally said. "I'll travel as far as Semna with you and then I will have to decide what I will do."

"I'll go back to Semna, too," said Hapu. "I'll report to the fort commander there and wait for another boat heading to Sai."

Ramose nodded. They were all going their separate ways, but, for a little while at least, they would be travelling together.

The three friends decided to walk to Semna rather than wait at the swollen river's edge in the hope of a boat passing by and stopping for them. Karoya hated sailing even when the river was at its calmest. She needed no encouragement to avoid it at a time of the worst inundation in fifty years. Hapu thought that he needed to get fit again after weeks of inactivity at the rebel fort. Ramose agreed with the plan. He didn't like to admit it, not even to himself, but he was happy to delay his return to the palace as much as possible.

They travelled early in the day and in the evening, resting during the hottest period of the day. The river provided fish as always. Karoya had a useful supply of grain. They collected whatever else they could as they walked through the barren rocky land towards Semna. It took them three and a half days. It wasn't an easy walk, but no one complained. They were all happy to postpone their separation. Ramose would never have guessed when he'd sailed by that desolate rocky land a month before that he would so soon have chosen to travel through it on foot. He could never predict what the gods had in store for him.

On the afternoon of the fourth day, the fort of Semna loomed on the opposite side of the river. There was a local boat that ferried people from one side of the swollen river to the other. Unfortunately, they had nothing with which to pay the boatman.

"But I'm Prince Ramose," Ramose insisted, wishing that just for once someone would believe him. "When I reach the other side, I can arrange to have you paid threefold."

The boatman refused to believe that Pharaoh's brother would be standing on a wharf in a dirty, ragged kilt and mended sandals without so much as a piece of copper. Hapu was threatening to send a battalion of soldiers over to sink his boat if he didn't take them across the river.

"I can pay for their passage," said a voice behind them.

The three friends all turned at once.

"Vizier Wersu!" said Ramose, his scowl transformed into a smile. "It's good to see a familiar face."

The confused boatman bowed down to the vizier. He'd never seen him before, but with his flowing robes and glittering medallion at least he looked like a vizier.

The vizier went across the river with them. It was a slow trip, but Ramose needed the whole passage to tell the vizier all his adventures. It wasn't until the boatman was tying up his craft that Ramose finally asked the vizier what he was doing in Semna.

The vizier hesitated before he answered. "A number of matters required us to come to Semna," he said. "Not the least being concern for your safety."

"So you got the letter from Kashta?" asked Ramose, puzzled that the letter had arrived so quickly.

"No, Highness," replied the vizier. "We left Thebes four weeks ago. We had not heard about your capture, but we did get news that the boat you were on had sunk and that no survivors had been found."

"Not entirely true as you see," said Ramose, smiling grimly.

"Look!"

Karoya and Ramose followed Hapu's pointing finger and saw a beautiful cedar boat moored downstream. The prow and stern curved up into elaborately carved papyrus stalks in flower. On the deck was a covered cabin, painted in red, blue and gold. It was the royal barge.

"His Majesty will be overjoyed to hear that you are safe," said the vizier.

"Is Pegget here in Semna?" asked Ramose.

"He is, Highness. He has come to dedicate the new temple to Ra here in Semna."

The vizier was staring out at the river as he spoke. Ramose suspected he wasn't telling him everything.

Inside the towering fort of Semna it was much the same as the fort they had visited at Buhen, except that where there had been a large open space for soldiers to exercise, here there was a pavilion. It was a huge structure made from many, many cubits of white linen. Coloured pennants fluttered from the tops of the gold-tipped poles. The simple mud brick buildings were not suitable for a visit from the pharaoh. The vizier escorted Ramose and his friends into the pavilion.

"If you wouldn't mind waiting here, Highness," said the vizier.

Ramose didn't much like being told to wait like a servant. After ten minutes had passed and he was still standing there, he turned to his friends.

"I'm not waiting around," he said crossly. "I'm going to find my brother."

He took three paces in the direction that the vizier had taken and then he came to an abrupt halt. Four palace guards marched out and stood to attention, barring his way. They were followed by servants who spread embroidered rugs on the earth floor and lit incense. They brought out an ornate throne-like chair and placed it on the central rug. Three men who Ramose recognised as ministers from Thebes emerged next and stood around the empty chair. Then six women, all elegantly dressed, came out and also took their places around the throne. Finally, a single figure drifted out dressed in an exquisite pleated gown with intricate embroidery around the hem. Ramose stared at the figure.

"Hatshepsut," he said.

"Ramose," replied the princess as she took her seat and her women arranged her gown. "I see you are as grubby and dishevelled as ever."

"I was expecting our brother," said Ramose, ignoring her comment.

"Pharaoh is busy rehearsing the ritual for the dedication of the temple."

"You don't seem surprised to see me. Even though it had been reported that I had drowned."

"You do have a habit of coming back from the dead." She glanced at Karoya and Hapu. "I see you have found your friends along the way."

Hapu and Karoya both bowed to the princess.

"I suppose you are planning to disappear to foreign lands again."

"No, sister," said Ramose. "I have had time to think about my responsibilities. I intend to return to Thebes so that I can serve our brother and Egypt."

The corners of Hatshepsut's mouth turned up. Ramose felt a cold chill run down his spine.

"I am most pleased to hear that you are keen to serve Egypt," she said. "The war with Naharin does not go well."

"I will undertake some military training, as you suggested."

"But I thought you were in favour of a non-military response to the uprising."

"If that is possible, yes."

"You remember my proposal with regard to the Naharini?"

Ramose felt like there was a noose tightening around his neck.

"I had forgotten about it until you reminded me. I've had other matters on my mind."

"Things have progressed since your sudden departure. Your betrothed, Princess Tiya, arrived in Thebes soon after you left, keen to renew your acquaintance."

Hapu and Karoya looked at Ramose.

"Your arrival is very timely, Ramose," continued Hatshepsut. "Here is the princess now."

The three friends turned together as the Naharini princess entered. Ramose's mouth fell open. Hapu gaped in astonishment. Karoya stifled a laugh.

The princess had none of the practised grace of Hatshepsut. She stomped out crossly and folded her arms. She muttered something in Naharini.

"What did she say?" whispered Hapu.

"Something about hating lettuce and cucumbers," said Ramose, who knew a little of the Naharini language.

Ramose stared at his betrothed. She was pretty even when she was pouting. She was dressed in the manner of the Naharin, which Ramose thought was quite attractive.

Her dress was midnight blue and caught in around the waist by a cord. She wore lots of beads, not in the form of jewellery, but sewn onto her dress. The princess had brown hair that fell in soft waves to her shoulders. Her eyes were a startling blue. Under one arm was tucked a cloth doll. The princess was, by Ramose's estimation, about seven years old.

10

THE BARBARIAN
PRINCESS

"IS THIS my husband?" asked the Naharini princess in broken Egyptian as she looked Ramose up and down with a scowl.

Hatshepsut gave a slight nod.

"I don't like him," said Princess Tiya. "He's dirty."

"Prince Ramose has just arrived after a long and dangerous journey, Princess," said Vizier

Wersu. "He was captured by rebels. He has not yet had time to bathe."

"I'd rather have a pet monkey," the princess said. "There are plenty of husbands in Naharin," she added knowledgeably, "but no monkeys."

Hapu and Karoya were trying not to laugh as the little princess turned and stomped out without another word.

Ramose raised an eyebrow. "I don't seem to have made much of an impression on my bride."

Hatshepsut glared at him. "I am not concerned about her feelings...or yours. This alliance will stop an outbreak of war to our north."

Ramose was about to speak again, when Tuthmosis rushed in, barefoot, with several servants trailing anxiously after him.

"Ramose, I'm so glad to see you," said the pharaoh. "I thought you were dead."

"Not this time, Pegget," said Ramose, hugging his brother.

"You must have more adventures to tell me about," said the boy as a servant knelt at his feet to put on his sandals and another one tried to comb his hair.

"I have. I'll tell you when we have our evening meal."

Hatshepsut stood up. "It's about time you accepted your duty to Egypt, Ramose," she said and left with her entourage.

The vizier led the travellers out of the pavilion.

"I'm afraid there are only soldiers' quarters available for you, Highness," he said apologetically, as they approached a low mud brick building.

"This is a commander's room," he said, stopping outside a door.

"It'll do fine, Vizier," said Ramose. "What about Hapu and Karoya?"

"I'll find a room for Karoya," said the vizier. "Hapu will have to report to the barracks."

A cool bath made Ramose feel better. He scrubbed off the dirt of the desert and put on a clean white kilt. His reflection looked back at him from a polished bronze mirror. He looked like a prince again. Now he had to act like one.

He was on his way to speak to the vizier, when his brother came tearing out of the royal apartments and raced straight past him. He was followed a few moments later by Princess Tiya, who was running full pelt after the young pharaoh.

"You can't catch me," shouted Tuthmosis.

"Yes I can," yelled the princess.

Ramose smiled and continued on his way. He found the vizier poring over a papyrus.

"Vizier Wersu," said Ramose, smiling at his friend. "You're hard at work I see."

The high spirits of the children had further improved Ramose's mood.

"This has just arrived from Libya," said the vizier, grim-faced and unaffected by Ramose's good humour. "The news is not good. We must send another battalion north immediately."

The vizier looked old and tired. He, more than anyone, was burdened with the weight of responsibility for Egypt and her people.

"At least you don't have to worry about Naharin," Ramose said, pulling up a stool and sitting next to the vizier. "Once Princess Tiya and I are married, there'll be peace with the Naharini."

Vizier Wersu looked at Ramose with relief.

"You intend to go ahead with the marriage?"

"It's my duty," replied Ramose.

The vizier's careworn mouth started to form a smile.

"I have one condition though."

The half-formed smile dissolved.

"I want my wife and I to live in the palace at Thebes. I have sworn to the gods that I will support and advise my brother. My first duty is to Pharaoh. I can't keep an eye on him if I'm in Naharin."

The vizier sighed. "Princess Hatshepsut will not like this arrangement."

"You'll have to make her like it, Vizier."

Ramose looked into the old man's watery eyes.

"Wersu, this marriage is a strategy, no different to attacking a city or capturing a fort. It will be more effective if the young princess lives in Egypt. She'll be a hostage. A spoilt and pampered one, but a hostage nonetheless."

"I will speak to Princess Hatshepsut," said the vizier, getting creakily to his feet. "She can not argue with the wisdom of your proposal."

Ramose smiled. "Good. Let's go and eat, then."

Karoya and Hapu were already in the pavilion, both washed and dressed in clean white clothing.

Hapu's eyes lit up when he saw the food that was being brought into the pavilion.

"This is better than soldier's rations," he said to Ramose, as servants surrounded him with food. "I'd marry a spoilt brat of a princess if I could eat like this every day."

Hapu piled his bowl with gazelle meat, vegetables and enough bread to feed six people. Princess Tiya was not so easy to please. She shook her pretty head at everything that was offered to her. An old woman, who Ramose guessed was the child's nanny, was trying hard to make her eat some beans. The princess picked up the beans and hurled them across the room. Some specially prepared meat was brought from the kitchens and she eventually settled down to eat.

"What a little monster your future wife is," said Hapu.

"She reminds me of myself when I was that age," said Ramose.

"You weren't such a brat, were you?"

"I'm afraid I was."

Tuthmosis gestured to Ramose to eat with him. Throughout the meal, Ramose kept an eye on Vizier Wersu who was in deep conversation with Hatshepsut. After everyone had finished eating, the vizier stood and asked for silence.

"I have an announcement to make," he said. "Prince Ramose and Princess Tiya will be married as soon as it can be arranged. The royal couple will live in the palace at Thebes."

"That sounds like a wonderful idea, Vizier Wersu," said Tuthmosis. "I'd like it if Tiya lived with us in Thebes."

The little princess was sulking again. "I want a pet monkey, not a husband."

"That will be my marriage gift to you," said Ramose graciously.

The princess's face broke into a smile. "All right. I'll marry you," she said. Everyone laughed. Everyone except Hatshepsut, who glared at Ramose.

"But before we return to Thebes and start planning the marriage," the vizier reminded them, "we must concentrate on our purpose here in Semna. We have a temple to dedicate to Ra."

The happy mood was contagious. Everyone in the royal pavilion smiled and laughed. Even the normally morose ministers managed to smile.

Dancers and musicians entertained the royal party. The little princess climbed up on the platform and played a game with Tuthmosis which involved throwing carved pieces of lapis lazuli in the air and seeing how many could be caught on the back of the hand.

Ramose went back to join his friends.

"We play a similar game in Kush," said Karoya as she watched the children play. "Except we use ordinary stones, not jewels."

The two children were laughing as they played.

"It's good to see Pegget happy," said Ramose.

The only one who hadn't caught the mood was Hatshepsut. She came up to Ramose.

"The Naharini king may not want his daughter living in Thebes," she said.

"That's why I'm writing to him personally and sending him a gift of twenty talents of gold," Ramose replied with a broad smile. "That should make the loss of his daughter less painful."

Hatshepsut left the pavilion without another word.

"I didn't expect your forthcoming marriage to make you so happy," said Hapu, as he got up to go to the barracks. "You've been smiling all evening."

"It's not the marriage that's making me happy. It's the fact that I've beaten Hatshepsut. There was nothing she could say against my proposal."

Ramose woke with his heart beating fast, as if a sudden noise had disturbed his sleep. He'd fallen asleep as soon as he lay down on the clean, white sheets. Now he was wide awake again.

He had the distinct impression that there was someone in the room. He listened. There was no sound. He sat up and looked around. Moonlight illuminated every corner of the simple room. It was empty.

The incident left him with an uneasy feeling that he couldn't shake. He couldn't get back to sleep. He rose as soon as it was light.

Ramose spread a sheet of papyrus on a low table and opened his battered pen box. Someone had filled it with fresh reeds.

"I thought I was up early," said Hapu as he poked his head around the door.

"I couldn't sleep. I have to write to the Naharini king."

Ramose picked up one of the reeds and chewed the end to make a brush.

"Yerck," he said, spitting out fibres of reed. "The reeds here in Semna taste worse than the reeds from Thebes. When I get back to the palace, I'm going to have a servant whose only job is to chew the end of my pens for me."

"I've joined a battalion that's going to Libya," said Hapu. "I have a few days leave before we depart though."

"You go and have breakfast. I'll join you later."

Ramose dipped his pen in a jar of water, rubbed it on his ink block and started to write. The letter took longer than he expected. He chose every word with care. He didn't want his future father-in-law to spoil his plan.

"You haven't had breakfast," said Karoya when she came to look for him over an hour later. "I brought you some bread and figs."

She handed him the food wrapped in a linen cloth.

"I'm not hungry," he said.

Karoya's brow creased. "You don't look well, Ramose."

"My stomach's a bit upset. It must have been the gazelle meat I ate at dinner last night."

He handed her the letter.

"Read this. Tell me if I sound like a dutiful son-in-law."

Karoya read the letter and gave it her approval.

There was a knock at the door and to Ramose's surprise Hatshepsut came in.

"I'd like to speak to you," she said, glancing pointedly at Karoya.

"You can speak in front of Karoya," he replied. "I have no secrets from her."

Hatshepsut stood in silent protest for a moment before she spoke.

"I wanted you to know, Ramose, that I am happy to have you stay at Thebes." She bowed her head slightly.

Ramose tried to hide his triumphant smile.

"In future, we must work together in our service to Egypt."

Hatshepsut held out a piece of papyrus. "Here is the marriage contract. Princess Tiya has already signed it."

Ramose quickly signed his name under the princess's crooked hieroglyphs.

"I have drawn up a list of important guests who must be invited to your wedding," continued Hatshepsut. "The King of Naharin of course, the leader of the Hyksos, the Syrian lords, our aunts in Memphis. I think it would be better if the invitations were written in your own hand."

"What about my terrible handwriting?" asked Ramose.

Hatshepsut smiled and picked up the letter that Ramose had written. "Your writing has improved somewhat," she said.

"I hope we will be friends again, Penu," Ramose said as Hatshepsut turned to leave. He couldn't remember the last time he'd called her by her pet name.

"I'm sure we will," she said, smiling at her brother. She ignored Karoya as she swept out of the room.

"I'm legally married now," he said to Karoya.

Karoya looked puzzled. "But the ceremony won't be for weeks."

"That's a formality. A chance for the people to celebrate. The signing of the contract is all that's really needed."

Ramose glanced at the list of wedding guests. "I think I'll rest this morning, until my stomach is feeling better. I'll make a start on these."

"I have to go and see the vizier," said Karoya. "He has an idea for a position for me."

Karoya left and Ramose wrote out two of the wedding invitations. His head was heavy. His stomach felt as if there was a granite block in it. He wrote another invitation and then lay down to rest.

He woke when Karoya returned. "You have missed the midday meal, Ramose," she said. "You haven't eaten all day."

Ramose couldn't lift his head from the mattress.

"What's wrong?" Karoya asked, looking at him anxiously. "You look terrible."

He felt terrible.

"Perhaps something has bitten me. A poisonous spider, a scorpion."

"What did you eat last night besides the gazelle?" Karoya asked.

"I can't remember."

"Think, Ramose, did you eat anything that was specially prepared for you? Did someone else pour you a drink?"

Ramose searched through his befuddled brain. He shook his head. "I ate from the same platter as my brother. I poured us both wine from the same jar." Ramose didn't understand why Karoya was quizzing him. He just wanted her to go away and let him sleep.

Karoya bent closer to look at him. "I think someone has poisoned you."

"No—"

Karoya didn't let him finish. "Open your mouth," she demanded. Ramose tried to object. Karoya put her fingers in his mouth and prised it open.

"There's a stain on your tongue, Ramose."

"Ink," he said.

Karoya shook her head. "Ink is black. The mark on your tongue is purple."

Ramose wasn't interested in what she was saying. He just wanted to be left in peace. He watched as she snatched up one of the unused reeds and scraped it on a piece of parchment. It left a purple mark. Ramose saw her leave the room. At last, he thought, I can rest. He closed his eyes.

The next thing he knew, Karoya was pulling him into a sitting position and making him drink something. Something that didn't taste good. She forced his head back and held his nose. Ramose had no choice but to swallow the foul-tasting stuff.

He was about to protest, when the walls started to circle his head and his stomach lurched and heaved in violent spasms. Next, he was vomiting into a basin that Karoya put in front of him. He had never been so sick in his life. He retched again and again, until there was nothing but green bile to bring up. Karoya gave him water to drink. He gulped it down and then vomited that up as well.

Finally the spasms in his stomach ceased. The room stopped spinning and his head began to clear. Everything suddenly came into sharp focus. His sister's visit. Her unspoken admission of defeat. Her compliment about his writing. He should have realised.

"The reeds have been dipped in poison," Karoya said, lying him back on the bed.

"Hatshepsut," Ramose whispered. He felt tears fill his eyes. "Just for a moment I thought that she might still care about me."

Karoya took his hand.

Ramose stayed in bed for the rest of the day. Karoya brought him some bread that she had baked herself and fruit she had picked. She sat with him while he rested, and turned away any vistors, telling them that he was suffering from a slight stomach upset.

Pale shafts of moonlight filtered through a grille in the ceiling. Ramose had slept for most of the day and now he was wide awake. He got up. Karoya was sleeping on a reed mat at the foot of the bed. He stepped over her and went outside. The royal pavilion was dazzling in the light of an almost full moon. Ramose walked out through the gateway of the fort. For once, the guard didn't challenge him, but bowed and let him pass.

Ramose walked along the river's edge in the direction of the new temple. The white stone glowed eerily in the moonlight. The statues were all finished now. The four seated pharaohs had boyish features but each had a bearded chin. They stared blankly ahead of them as if they were trying to see something on the other side of the river. The fast-flowing waters of the Nile rushed by their stony feet. When the inundation had receded, the banks of the river would be thirty cubits away. Now, with the river level at its highest in living memory, it covered the first steps leading up to the temple.

The temple was cut from the natural rock of the river valley. The four enormous statues towered above him as he approached the gateway to the temple. His head didn't even reach their knees.

The moon was so bright that he could easily make out the carvings on the outer wall. One showed Tuthmosis, depicted as a fully grown man, with his foot on the head of an enemy. In another, he was bowing before a hawk-headed figure of Ra. Ramose walked to the gateway. A sleepy guard stirred as he approached. Ramose turned away and went down the steps to the edge of the rushing waters.

"The guard would have let you in, if you'd asked," said a voice behind him.

Ramose smiled without turning. It was Karoya. "I'm not in the mood for confronting guards."

Ramose sat down on one the steps. Karoya came and sat next to him.

"I thought I'd managed to creep out without waking you," he said.

"I wasn't asleep."

The two friends sat without speaking. The silence was disturbed only by the rush of the river and the yowl of a nearby cat.

Karoya broke the silence. "You can't stay in the palace at Thebes, Ramose. It's too dangerous."

"I have to. When the sun disappeared that day in the gold mine, I promised Ra I would do my duty to Egypt and to my brother." His voice had a hollow, defeated sound to it.

"You can't watch over Pharaoh if you're dead," Karoya said quietly.

"I'll be careful."

"You will have to have all your food tested. You will need a trusted bodyguard at all times," replied Karoya. "You can't be on the alert every minute of the day. Sooner or later you will relax your guard. Hatshepsut won't rest until you're dead. You might as well jump in the river now."

Ramose stared miserably at the shimmering river. He threw a stalk of grass into the water, watching as it was dragged below the surface by the swirling current.

Then he turned to his friend. His face brightened. "You're right. I'd be better off dead."

"I didn't mean it," said Karoya.

"You've given me an idea. I'll need your help though. And Hapu's."

11

WATERY GRAVE

RAMOSE decided that if he was going to go through with his plan, he had to do it quickly before he lost his nerve. The temple dedication was to be the following night. It would be the perfect time. Throughout the day he and his friends made preparations in secret.

As evening approached, Ramose made the crossing from the opposite side of the river in a barge decorated with blue lotus flowers. It had a Horus eye painted on either side of the prow. The barge was carrying a statue of Ra which had been carved out of pink granite from a quarry at Aswan. The statue lay in the middle of the barge, as if it was sleeping, nestled in a bed of straw, held in place by wooden rails. Either side of the reclining god were the rowers' benches. The rowers, including Hapu, bent forward and rocked back as they guided the boat to the western shore.

Ramose was seated just behind Hapu at Ra's feet. As Pharaoh's brother, he had the role of protecting Ra on his journey across the river. Three priests sat at the prow of the boat chanting hymns and throwing flowers into the river. Above them, a perfectly white sail strained at the mast as it caught the full strength of the wind. It was the wind that was doing most of the work in carrying the boat across the river. With the sail at the right angle, the northerly wind could be used to propel the boat from the eastern side of the river to the western side.

As they got closer to the shore, Ramose could see that torches had been set up along the river bank. It wasn't dark yet, so the flames looked pale and ineffective against the blue sky. A group of people stood on the steps of the temple, ready to welcome Ra to his new home.

Tuthmosis and the high priest were on the highest step. Hatshepsut stood a few steps down from the pharaoh. The vizier was alongside her with Princess Tiya. Three more priests were gathered on the bottom step, their sandals splashed by the rushing waters. They were waiting to carry the statue through the courtyard, through the halls and into a shrine deep inside the rock-cut temple. The priests would live in the temple for the rest of their lives. Each day, they would worship the god and make offerings to him.

Once a year, on a special feast day, they would carry Ra out of the temple so that the people could see him. Pharaoh was the only person besides the priests who could enter the inner shrine.

As the boat got closer to the western bank, a promontory of rock loomed towards them. It was time to put the plan into action. Ramose suddenly stood up.

"Sit down, Prince Ramose," said the boatman anxiously. "It's dangerous to stand. In a moment we'll…"

The rush of wind suddenly died as the boat sailed into the shelter of the rock promontory. The sail fell limply to the mast. The current caught the boat and pulled it sideways, causing it to rock alarmingly. Ramose lost his balance and tumbled into the turbulent waters. As he hit the water, Ramose heard Hapu's voice shouting to the other rowers.

"Don't stop. Keep rowing," he yelled, "or Ra will be lost in the waters as well."

Ramose took a deep breath as the current pulled him under. Then all he could hear was the rush of the river. He didn't fight against the tugging waters though, he let them carry him. He felt around his waist. There was a rope tied around him. He was frightened, but he held his breath and held on to the rope. Hapu had the other end tied securely around him. It was all part of the plan.

The rope suddenly yanked taut and Ramose stopped moving with the current. He opened his eyes. He peered through the water, thick with the silt washed down by the floods. He closed his eyes again and struck out in the direction of the bank. The plan that he'd hastily formulated during the day suddenly seemed rather rash. It was taking longer than he'd thought. He pushed his way to the surface and gulped in a mouthful of air and then plunged below again. He swam across the current, making slow progress, but with the rope stopping him from being washed further downstream. Then he felt the riverbed beneath his feet. He was close to the shore. He peered through the murky water. He could just make out a square shape. That was where he was heading. It was a drain from the temple. When the river level returned to normal, this would be high and dry on the riverbank. At the moment, it was about three cubits below the surface. The drain was big enough for him to crawl up. All he had to do was get to it. Only the first couple of cubits would be underwater. Then he'd be able to follow the drain up into the temple to where Karoya would be waiting. From the shore it would look like he'd never resurfaced. Everybody would think that he had drowned.

The rope yanked him to a halt again. The drain opening was still about four cubits away. They had only been able to estimate where the boat would be when it sailed into the shelter of the rock outcrop. Hapu had thought it would be further south. The rope was too short. It was also tugging him back the way he'd come. That meant the boat was moving again. The decision had been made that Ra was more important than Ramose.

The current wasn't so strong near the shore. Ramose could stand on the river bed without being dragged off his feet. He risked another mouthful of air and then yanked the rope three times. That was the signal that he'd safely reached the drain. The rope went slack. Hapu had let go of his end. Ramose was on his own. He moved cautiously towards the square shape that was the drain opening. It wasn't far—a little more than two cubits now. Three steps and he'd be there. He clutched at the edges of the stone drain. His fingers were cold. He couldn't grab hold. A sudden swirl in the water knocked him off his feet and carried him downstream. He watched in terror as his only escape from the tugging waters of the Nile slipped into the distance.

He remembered when he had thought he was about to drown before. This time Hapu wasn't going to appear and pull him from the water. Something scratched against his threshing arms. It was a branch, the branch of a tree submerged by the floods. He reached out. He grasped at the branch, but only caught a handful of soggy twigs which broke off in his hand. The force of the current grew stronger. He would never be able to swim back against it. His lungs were about to burst. The plan had failed. He was supposed to be faking his own drowning, but it looked like he would be drowning for real.

He suddenly jerked to a stop. The rope, still tied around his waist, had snagged on a submerged tree. He clambered among its branches, pulling himself hand over hand back towards the drain, fighting the urge to breathe in. When he ran out of tree branches, he pulled himself along holding onto sunken papyrus reeds. The drain came back into view. He grasped hold of the stone rim of the drain and pushed himself inside it. Everything was black. His relief turned to panic. He felt the sides of the narrow drain close around him. He was wedged tight and his empty lungs forced him to take a breath, even though he knew that he'd only be breathing in water.

Ramose lay on cold stone. Hands gently turned him over, then thumped him hard on the back. He coughed up slimy water. He took a deep breath. This time he breathed in incense-laden air.

"I told you this was a bad plan," whispered Karoya.

"Ouch," he yelped. Her hands were gentle but whatever it was she was using to bathe the cuts on his arms stung.

"The plan worked, didn't it?" said Ramose, getting up onto one elbow.

"Only just. If I hadn't climbed down into the drain and pulled you out when you passed out, you would have drowned."

Ramose sat up. They were deep inside the temple, in a small room that would soon be where the priests bathed to purify themselves before taking part in the daily rituals for Ra.

"I have everything you asked for," Karoya said. "A spare kilt, a water bag, scribal tools, a cloak."

"What about the gold?"

"I have gold." She pulled aside a fold of the cloak and revealed six large gold rings. "There's some copper as well."

"And no one saw you? I don't want to have to come and free you from prison."

"No one saw me." She smiled. "I am a good thief."

Karoya gave Ramose some bread and dried fish.

"Are you sure this is what you want to do?" she asked.

"I'm sure. The only way I can be safe from Hatshepsut's schemes is to be dead."

"How can you advise Pharaoh if he thinks you're dead?"

"I'll devise some way of getting messages to him. Perhaps he'll be visited by his dead brother in his dreams or maybe the gods will leave mysterious messages. When he's older, I'll let him know."

"It seems a high price for you to pay, living in exile again."

Ramose shook his head. "I don't think so. Some of my happiest memories are from when I was 'dead'."

Karoya smiled. "This will be different. You won't have Hapu and me to look after you."

Ramose's smile faded. "So, you're not coming to Thebes? I thought Vizier Wersu offered you a position as assistant to the assistant of the foreign minister."

"He did. I turned it down. I have spent enough time serving Egypt."

Ramose smiled sadly. Karoya deserved her freedom.

"Will you return to Kush?" he finally asked.

Karoya nodded.

"I don't suppose I will see you again, then."

"Who knows what the gods have in store for us?"

Ramose wasn't prepared to even guess.

"We have to let Hapu know I got to shore safely."

Karoya nodded. "I'll do that."

Ramose was about to object.

"You've got this far, you don't want to risk getting caught now. You stay here and rest." She wrapped her head-cloth around her head and silently crept out of the room.

Ramose lay back on the stone slab. He pictured the dedication ceremony. The boat would reach the shore and be securely tied up. The high priest would lead the procession into the temple as the statue was carried through the hall. The rest of the party would follow behind with their heads bowed. At the door of the inner shrine, the ministers, the vizier and the princesses would have to stop. Only Pharaoh and the priests would accompany Ra to his final home. Hapu would be back at the boat with the other rowers, anxiously waiting for a signal from Karoya that Ramose was safe. It hadn't been such a bad plan after all.

Karoya returned after a few minutes. "All is well," she said. "I saw Hapu."

"Good," said Ramose. "How is my brother?"

"He is very distressed. He thinks he has lost you again."

"I wish I could let him know I'm okay," Ramose said sadly. This was the only part of the plan he didn't like. "What about Princess Tiya?"

"Oh, she seemed upset, but when the vizier told her that she could still have a pet monkey, she soon cheered up."

Ramose smiled. "I hope that Tiya stays at the palace. She's a good companion for Pegget."

The two friends sat together through the hours of the night. When the oil lamp flickered out, they each picked up their reed bags and silently made their way out of the temple. The sounds of the exhausted priests, still chanting prayers to Ra, drifted through the corridors with the scent of incense. Ramose and Karoya slipped past the sleeping guard and out onto the steps. The first light was only just starting to bleach the darkness on the horizon. The royal party had long gone. The only remains of the ceremony were a few lotus petals lying on the steps.

Ramose and Karoya made their way up the craggy slope behind the temple. Suddenly Karoya pulled Ramose to the ground.

"There's someone down by the river."

In the dim light, Ramose could make out the figure of a young woman standing at the river's edge.

"It's Hatshepsut," he whispered.

His sister was standing alone, barefoot, wearing a simple linen shift that came only to her knees. She wore no jewellery, no crown. A breeze lifted her hair from her shoulders. She could have been any Egyptian girl. She knelt and picked up a handful of lotus petals and then threw them into the river.

"That's for you," whispered Karoya.

Ramose nodded. "She's chosen a lonely path," he said. "No one will dare to get close to her."

Crouched on the hillside, he watched his sister return to the fort. "Let's go," he said.

They climbed for half an hour. When they reached the top of the hill, they turned and saw the rim of the sun break over the horizon. The sky turned orange, the colour of the fruit that Ramose had eaten in foreign lands. The rays of sunlight lit the seated pharaohs.

"Ra has survived another journey through the underworld."

"So have you, Ramose," replied Karoya.

"This is where we must part."

Karoya shook her head. "I've changed my mind. I'm not going to Kush."

Ramose looked at her, puzzled.

"Hapu and I decided that you'll starve if you don't have someone to bake bread for you. I'm coming with you to Thebes."

Ramose felt as if an enormous burden had been lifted from his shoulders.

"Hapu has arranged with the vizier that once he has finished his service in Libya, he will become palace guard. So he can become your eyes and ears in the palace."

"But I thought you weren't willing to serve Egypt any longer?"

"Who said anything about serving? Someone with such terrible handwriting as you will make a miserable living as a scribe. We will work as scribes together."

She handed him the bag containing his scribal tools and the gold and copper. "Here. You carry this."

Ramose smiled at Karoya. He lifted the bag onto his shoulder and they walked together towards Thebes.

A WORD FROM THE AUTHOR

Everybody seems to have trouble pronouncing Ramose's sister's name. It's actually very easy—Hat-shep-sut (I sometimes wish I'd spelt it with hyphens in the book to save all the confusion!). Like Prince Ramose, Hatshepsut was a real person. Whereas history has recorded almost nothing about Ramose, it has told us a lot about Hatshepsut. In ancient Egypt only men could become Pharaoh. Hatshepsut decided to change that. She wanted to be Pharaoh. It didn't happen overnight. She spent many years as queen to Pharaoh Tuthmosis II and co-regent to Tuthmosis III before she became Pharaoh.

Some readers have told me they didn't like the way that I made Hatshepsut turn out to be a bad person. I felt that to be so determined to become Pharaoh, so hungry for power, she'd have had to have been very strong-willed and ruthless. If you have any comments or questions about the Ramose books, I'd love to hear from you. Email me at carole@bdb.com.au

This is the fourth and final book in the Ramose series. That doesn't mean I won't still think about what happens to Ramose next. In a way a story never really ends. Now it's your turn to imagine what happened to Ramose in the rest of his life.

GLOSSARY

acacia

A type of small tree that grows in dry areas.

akhet

The ancient Egyptians divided the year into three seasons. Akhet was the first season of the year, when the Nile flooded.

Amun

The king of the Egyptian gods during the New Kingdom period.

barbarian

A person who belongs to a group of people that is considered to be primitive or uncivilised.

besieged

When a town or castle or fort is surrounded by enemy troops.

carnelian

An orangey-red stone used in jewellery.

cataract

A place where a river falls to a lower level in a waterfall or rapids.

cornflower

A tall herb plant with bright blue flowers.

crook and flail

The pharaoh carries these. They are symbols of kingship. The crook is a short metal rod with a hooked end. The flail is a metal rod with strands of leather hanging from the top.

cubit

The cubit was the main measurement of distance in ancient Egypt. It was the average length of a man's arm from his elbow to the tips of his fingers, 52.4 cm.

ebony

Wood from a particular tree. It is a hardwood that is black and used for making furniture.

frankincense

A type of incense that is made from gum from a special type of tree that grows in Asia and Africa.

goblet

A bowl-shaped drinking cup with a long stem and a base.

gourd

The dried shell of a melon or similar vegetable, used as a bowl to eat or drink from.

Great Place

The name ancient Egyptians gave to the valley near Thebes where pharaohs were buried. Today we call it the Valley of the Kings.

griffin

A mythical monster which has the body of a lion and the head and wings of an eagle.

hieroglyphs

A system of writing used by the ancient Egyptians.

Horus

The Egyptian god of the sky.

jackal

A type of wild dog that lives in Africa and Asia.

jasper

A dark green gemstone.

lapis lazuli

A dark-blue semi-precious stone which the Egyptians considered to be more valuable than any other stone because it was the same colour as the heavens.

mirage

A false image of a sheet of water caused by light being distorted by very hot air in the desert or on a hot road.

nomads

A tribe of people who have no permanent home. They wander from place to place according to the seasons and food supplies.

oracle

A person who can tell what is going to happen in the future.

palm-width

The average width of the palm of an Egyptian man's hand, 7.5 centimetres.

papyrus

A plant with tall, triangular-shaped stems that grows in marshy ground. Ancient Egyptians made a kind of paper from the dried stems of this plant.

Pharaoh

The title of the ancient kings of Egypt.

pylon

A gateway with towers on either side that get narrower towards the top. There is often a pylon gateway into an Egyptian temple.

prow

The front part of a boat or ship.

pyramid

A massive structure built of stone with a square base and four sloping sides that meet at a point. The pyramids were built as royal tombs for the pharaohs and their families.

quay

A place where ships can tie up and unload their passengers or cargo.

sceptre

A rod held by a king or queen as a symbol of royal power.

scribe

A person who makes a living by writing. Scribes wrote things for people who could not write. Before printing was invented they copied documents.

scorpion

A small animal with a pair of pincers (like a crab) and a long curly tail which has a sting in the end of it. The stings of some scorpions are fatal to humans.

senet

A board game played by ancient Egyptians. It involved two players each with seven pieces and was played on a rectangular board divided into thirty squares. Archaeologists have found many senet boards in tombs, but haven't been able to work out what the rules of the game were.

shrine

A box or a chest made to hold a sacred object.

sphinx

An Egyptian stone statue of a creature with the head of a person and the body of an animal. Usually they have the head of a pharaoh and the body of a seated lion.

tamarisk

A type of tree with feathery pink or white flowers.

turquoise

A greenish-blue precious stone.

underworld, afterlife

The ancient Egyptians believed that the earth
was a flat disc. Beneath the earth was the
underworld, a dangerous place. Egyptians
believed that after they died they had to pass
through the underworld before they could live forever in the afterlife.

vizier

A very important person in ancient Egypt. He was
the pharaoh's chief minister who helped with the
government of Egypt.

WHERE TO FROM HERE?

IF you want to find out more about ancient Egypt, here are a few suggestions about how to get started.

The Internet: here are three great web sites that will give you lots of information about the lives and customs of ancient Egyptians.

http://guardians.net/egypt/kids

http://interoz.com/egypt/kids

www.clpgh.org/cmnh/exhibits/egypt

The library: there are lots of books about all aspects of life in ancient Egypt. You can look up this subject under 932 in the library. Here are a few titles to start with.

Peter Clayton, *Family Life in Ancient Egypt*, Hodder

Geraldine Harris and Delia Pemberton, *The British Museum Illustrated Encyclopaedia of Ancient Egypt*, British Museum Press

Lesley Sims, *Usborne Time Tours—Visitors Guide to Ancient Egypt*, Usborne

SOME GODS OF ANCIENT EGYPT

Amun
The king of the Egyptian gods.

Hapi
The god of the Nile.

Horus
The god of the sky.

Maat
The goddess of justice.

Osiris
The god of the underworld.

Seth
The god of chaos and confusion also the god of the desert and foreign lands.

Thoth
The god of the moon also the god of writing.